June Andrade
& The Boys

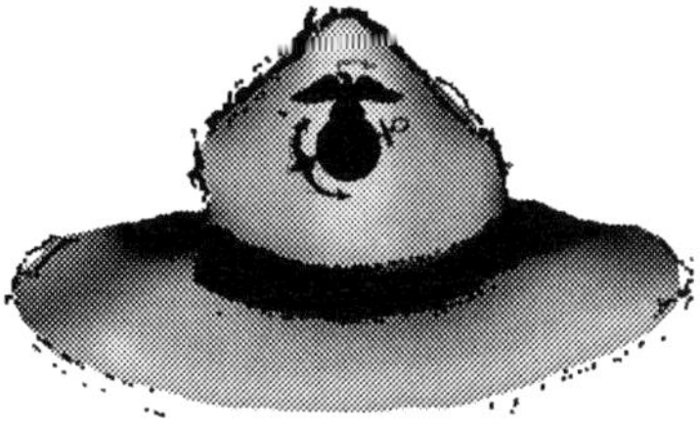

THE HAT and THE CAT

June Andrade

Illustrations by Liesl Bell

ISBN 0-7414-4679-0

Published by:

INFINITY
PUBLISHING.COM

1094 New DeHaven Street, Suite 100
West Conshohocken, PA 19428-2713
Info@buybooksontheweb.com
www.buybooksontheweb.com
Toll-free (877) BUY BOOK
Local Phone (610) 941-9999
Fax (610) 941-9959

Printed in the United States of America

Printed on Recycled Paper

Published April 2008

Dedicated to:

The committed Marine Corps Recruiters
who are devoted to finding those
precious young Americans who will
answer the call to become one of

A FEW GOOD MEN!

and

The magnificent Marine Corps Drill
Instructors who, proudly and meticulously,
weave the fabric of America's youth into

THE FEW, THE PROUD, THE MARINES!

With thanks and gratitude for your service,

June Andrade

TABLE OF CONTENTS

THE FORMING

PHASE ONE

PHASE TWO

PHASE THREE

Chapter 1

AN UNINVITED GUEST

Thursday, 12:02 a.m.

When the solitary tomcat topped the Marine Crossing Bridge, he could barely see the sentry stationed at the Parris Island main gate. “Bless the fog,” he purred. “A good night for prowling around the base.” The sentry blinked and Tomcat Pepper Parker came aboard—into someone else’s territory.

Having accomplished his first mission, the panther-like black cat inched along his well-worn path beside the salt marsh, hissing at the swarms of no-see-em sand fleas dedicated to the task of eating him alive. Pepper flicked his ears in protest and swished his long tail, trying to rid himself of the vicious pests. Exasperated, he paused and mentally opened his secret pocket. The large invisible pocket was located on one side of his stomach and contained what the huge tomcat considered to be his ‘essentials.’ He reached in, careful not to disturb his friend, Mister Mouse, or his stash of catnip, and took out his trusty flask of SOS bug spray. After he had covered himself from top to tail with the sweet-smelling liquid, the pesky flying teeth swarmed off in the opposite direction. “Dang-it,” he hissed, “I should have refilled it before I left home; but this little dab should do me for tonight.”

With the no-see-ems redirected, the tomcat replaced the flask and launched himself again toward his target: Recruit Receiving. Pepper’s cousin Danny Parker would be arriving on the bus from Savannah at exactly 1:50 a.m. He had been very specific about the time, and Pepper didn’t want to miss him.

The huge cat kept to the edge of the salt marsh, picking his way through dead spartina grass and the pulsing pluff mud sucking at his paws, seeming to come alive with fiddler crabs scurrying sideways at his approach.

As he began to climb out of the aromatic marsh, Pepper paused to watch a great blue heron and a snowy egret snapping up tasty morsels of fish from the inlet waterway, and then scampered over Archer’s Creek Bridge to the sanctuary of Horse Island. He raced through the traffic circle, past the picnic tables and onto Boulevard de France, another causeway lined with palmetto trees.When a lone car approached from behind, Pepper disappeared behind one of the nearby trees. The sedan slowed as it moved past the area where the military police thought they had sighted movement—possibly a misguided recruit, but probably just a raccoon. They drove on slowly as the dense fog closed in silently behind them.

Taking a shortcut, the cat was just a blur zipping behind the commissary and dental office. He arrived at his destination with time to spare, time he would spend cleaning off the stinky mud.

Before attempting the big clean-up, Pepper investigated the area surrounding Recruit Receiving for possible hiding places and other spectators who might be a threat. Pinky Possum, her four babies hanging from her tail, trotted across the clearing just as Ricky Raccoon surfaced from the trash can, covered in bits of pizza and white Styrofoam pellets. He looked like a snowball with red eyes as he scurried under a nearby oleander bush. The only real item of interest to the cat was the rows of yellow footprints on the pavement in front of the door to Recruit Receiving. Very interesting—but not a threat. Satisfied that the territory was secure, Pepper stationed himself just outside the lighted area, and the clean-up began.

While the big cat groomed himself, he had flashbacks to where he had spent the earlier part of the evening. He and his brother Bubba Billy had gone to Madam MoJoe's barrier island near Tanzi to listen and learn about some new defensive techniques. They already knew how to make themselves appear larger by stretching their bodies and puffing up. Tonight they had learned about inside sheaths that would hold their tails alongside their spine, allowing them to walk upright on their hind legs for long periods of time. Also, they had learned how to retract their whiskers. One never knew when a good old-fashioned catfight might break out; the whiskers would be safe in their sheaths. He and the other whiskered Pet Pals hadn't been aware of the sheaths or how to exercise control over them. It had been a very eventful evening so far, and the best was yet to come—a party at Fourth Battalion. But first he needed to catch a quick catnap and rest after his long trek from the islands.

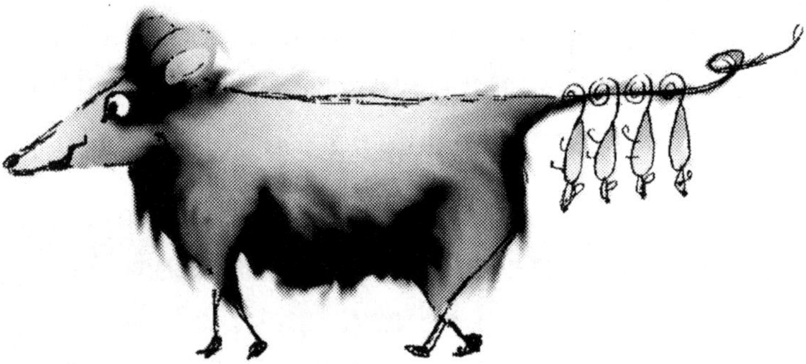

Chapter 2

INCOMING!

Thursday, 1:30 a.m.

The bus glided under the billboard-size sign spanning Boulevard de France that proclaimed, PARRIS ISLAND: WHERE THE DIFFERENCE BEGINS.

At exactly 1:50 a.m. the bus arrived with its precious cargo of new recruits. After pulling up in front of the red brick building, the bus stopped, and its doors opened with a whoosh and a sigh. Mission accomplished, the driver left the bus.

At that precise moment the door to the building marked Recruit Receiving banged open, and what the young civilians on the bus feared most became a reality. Silent prayers and loud vocal pleas of, "Oh God, please help me!" and "What in the world have I done, and how am I going to get out of this mess?" permeated the air of the bus.

Pepper came closer and watched as an enormous Marine alpha male, wearing a camouflage uniform and dark brown campaign hat, charged out of the building toward the bus, vaulted up the steps and yelled, without even a how-do-you-do, NOW! EVERYBODY GET OFF MY BUS! GET RID OF WHATEVER YOU'RE CHEWING, EATING, OR SMOKING AND GET OFF MY BUS! NOW! MOVE IT! MOVE IT NOW!

Pepper soon lost track of who was getting off the bus, because the Marine wannabes were scrambling all over each other, but he was sure he hadn't seen Danny. His cousin must have fallen asleep and needed a wake-up call. "I can handle that," smirked Pepper. "I'll just slap him upside the head and invite him to the ladies' party over at Fourth Battalion after he's finished here." Sneaking past the drill instructor onto the bus was easy, because the alpha male was distracted, screaming at the bunch of sleepy civilians and herding them onto those rows of yellow footprints on the pavement.

As Pepper hurried down the aisle of the bus looking for Danny, his whiskers snapped, crackled and popped, signifying DANGER! The Drill Instructor had suddenly materialized behind him and was yelling, YOU! I TOLD YOU TO GET OFF MY BUS! NOW! MOVE IT! GET OFF MY BUS!

Pepper lost all interest in finding Cousin Danny. His only concern now was survival, and that meant doing what he was told and doing it NOW! Being one himself, the cat understood the alpha male's power that demanded instant obedience and respect from others within his territory—and this was definitely THE MAN'S territory. Instinctively, a rush of adrenalin raced through his system, igniting the defensive enlargement of his body and retraction of his tail and whiskers. He was now a mere "Bravo" cat or—in the Drill Instructor's opinion—not even a lowly "Zulu," which was the bottom of the alphabet!

Once off the bus and onto the set of yellow footprints, Pepper tried to disappear behind the nearest Marine wannabe.

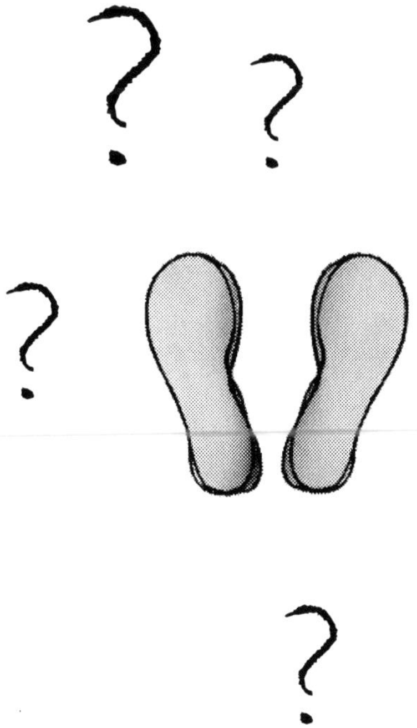

WE MAKE MARINES

Chapter 3

A BIG CASE OF MISTAKEN IDENTITY

"Mr. Drill Instructor," cried Pepper, "What we have here is a failure to communicate! I AM NOT A MARINE RECRUIT! I DIDN'T ENLIST! I'M A FELINE, NOT A FEMALE! I'VE BEEN CATNAPPED, AND SOMEBODY'S GONNA PAY!"

ARE YOU THREATENING ME, RECRUIT? screamed the stunned drill instructor.

"NO SIR!" shouted the cat. You should be looking for my cousin Danny! He's probably still asleep on the bus! That's my story, and I'm sticking to it! It's so simple—all you have to do is call my mistress, Jessie Lee Parker; she'll vouch for me! She needs me, and she'll be worried if I don't come home! MEOW-OW-OW!"

SO, RECRUIT! YOU HAVE A MISTRESS! THAT MEANS YOU MUST BE CHEATING ON YOUR WIFE!

"You think I'm cheating on my wife?" exclaimed the incredulous Pepper. "Well, Mister Smarty Pants, for your information I'm not married! Felines don't get married… unless you count the rich Hollywood types.

"What planet are you from, Mister?" inquired Pepper. "Just about everyone in Beaufort and even lots of faraway places knows Jessie Lee! She's been there or done that too many times to count! I'm not at liberty to tell you where she's been or what she did when she got there, so don't ask!"

SHUT YOUR FACE RECRUIT! YOU ARE ON MY ISLAND AND YOU WILL DO EXACTLY WHAT YOU ARE TOLD AND YOU WILL DO IT NOW!

"That's nice, Your Honor; I appreciate your diligence, but you don't need to worry about me, and you don't need to shout! So, if it's not too much trouble, I'll need a ride home now. Or maybe I could just pussyfoot off into the fog, disappear, and we'll just forget about this terrible little misunderstanding. Besides, there's somewhere I need to be, and it's way past my snack time."

LISTEN UP! roared the drill instructor. NOW! I'LL TELL YOU WHERE YOU GO, WHEN YOU GO, AND WHAT YOU'LL DO WHEN YOU GET THERE, UNDERSTAND? UNDERSTAND? I CAN'T H-E-A-R-R YOU!

Fuming at the smallest recruit, he bellowed,

LOUDER, LITTLE MOUSE, CAT GOT YOUR TONGUE?

"Okay," agreed Pepper, "if I can't have a snack, how about a phone call? Even the Beaufort Police will allow one call."

Pepper smirked as he punched in the numbers, confident that Jessie Lee would rescue him, and the dressing-down she would give the drill instructor would be music to his ears. He could hardly wait to hear her sweet voice. "Rats! The answering machine! Hello, Jessie Lee, this is Pepper. I arrived safely at Parris Island. I'll write to you as soon as I can. Do not send me any treats in the mail. That's all for now, bye-bye."

DID I HEAR YOU SAY 'BYE-BYE' RECRUIT? the man in the big brown hat asked. DID I TELL YOU TO SAY 'BYE-BYE?' DID I? DID I? BIG BOYS DON'T SAY 'BYE- BYE' TO THEIR MOMMIES! YOU WILL ALWAYS ADDRESS A WOMAN AS MA'AM! DO YOU UNDERSTAND?

"Whatever," hissed the annoyed cat. "Now, Mister Person-in-Charge, please point me in the direction of the little recruit's room. It's kind of an emergency. And while I'm gone, would you please turn off those bright lights?"

The drill instructor's eyes bulged out so far Pepper

thought for sure they'd just pop right out, bounce off the floor and possibly execute a little dance.

'I', the Hat shouted, 'I' IS NOT IN YOUR VOCABULARY, RECRUIT! UNTIL I TELL YOU OTHERWISE, YOU WILL REFER TO YOURSELF AS "THIS RECRUIT!" UNDERSTAND? UNDERSTAND? I CAN'T H-E-A-R-R YOU!

"There IS no 'I'? 'I' is gone? Where did 'I' go?" inquired Pepper.

In a voice that rocked the room, the furious drill instructor responded, 'I' IS BACK HOME WITH HIS MOMMIE, RECRUIT! 'I' IS SITTING IN FRONT OF MOMMIE'S TELEVISION WATCHING CARTOONS, EATING MOMMIE'S ICE CREAM! IS THAT WHERE YOU ARE RECRUIT? NO! YOU ARE ON MY BASE, OBEYING MY RULES, AND YOUR BUTT BELONGS TO ME UNTIL THE MARINE CORPS TELLS ME DIFFERENT! UNDERSTOOD? I CAN'T H-E-A-R-R YOU!

"Didn't I tell you I'm not the cat you're looking for?" asked Pepper. "That would be my double-crossing cousin from up north! He's the one you really want, and he's still on the bus waiting for you."

The drill instructor had had enough of the sassy recruit. In a deadly whisper, he said, RECRUIT, WE HAVE PAPERS ON YOU FROM THE MARINE

CORPS RECRUITER IN WESTFIELD, MASSACHUSETTS. SO EXPLAIN TO ME HOW YOU'RE HERE IF YOU'RE STILL ON THE BUS!

"Recruiters make mistakes, and this is a big one," growled Pepper. "I'm a cat! Cats rule! Hear me roar!!!"

RECRUIT, warned the drill instructor, BECAUSE THE COMMANDANT DOESN'T ALLOW US TO USE TIME OUTS OR NAUGHTY CHAIRS, YOU HAVE RACKED UP TWENTY MINUTES OF QUARTERDECKING TIME TO BE EXECUTED AFTER YOUR PICK-UP! IS THAT CLEAR?

"Clear as a bell! That's a deal I can live with," said Pepper, thinking he had won the war of words with the disagreeable drill instructor.

Pepper wasn't interested in the quarterdeck threat, because he felt confident that he would be rescued long before then. But the idea of being "picked up" could prove interesting. Maybe he would just hang out to see what the ladies looked like....

Chapter 4

ASH AND TRASH

As the drill instructor again screamed for everyone to LISTEN UP, he gave each recruit a brown paper bag for clothes and jewelry. At the same time a large orange crate was wheeled into the room, and the Man in the Hat shouted, THIS IS YOUR LAST CHANCE TO COME CLEAN! GET RID OF STUFF LIKE GUM, KNIVES, CIGARETTES, FOOD, DICE, CARDS, DRUGS, LIQUIDS, PICTURES OF YOUR GIRLFRIEND, YOUR BUDDY'S GIRLFRIEND, YOUR MOTHER, YOUR DOG, ET CETERA!

Pepper didn't have anything he considered "stuff" he wanted to be rid of, but he made a note to look for some "et cetera" on his next trip to downtown Beaufort. For now, he would just try to hold onto his mouse and the stash of catnip he had hidden away in his secret pocket. If Cousin Danny didn't show up, he could always use them to trade for favors.

Leaving no room for doubt, the drill instructor advised the recruits, YOU ARE NOT AT HOME! DO YOU UNDERSTAND ME?

SIR, YES SIR! replied the recruits.

YOU WILL NOW MEMORIZE THESE TWO ARTICLES OF THE UNIFORM CODE OF MILITARY JUSTICE, ALSO KNOWN AS THE U-C-M-J:

FIRST: YOU MAY NOT STRIKE A MARINE.

SECOND: IF YOU RUN AWAY, YOU ARE SUBJECT TO MILITARY LAW.

EVERYTHING YOU DO WILL BE DONE QUICKLY AND LOUDLY. DO YOU UNDERSTAND ME? I CA-A-N'T HEAR YOU!

SIR, YES SIR! screamed the Marine wannabes.

The drill instructor continued, YOU HAVE EACH BEEN HANDED A COPY OF YOUR GENERAL ORDERS. YOU WILL MEMORIZE EACH ONE. WHEN YOU ARE OLD AND ON YOUR DEATH BED, YOU WILL STILL BE ABLE TO RECITE THEM IF THE BIG DRILL INSTRUCTOR IN THE SKY ASKS YOU TO!

BEGINNING NOW AND FOR THE DURATION OF YOUR TIME IN MY MARINE CORPS, YOU WILL DISCONTINUE CIVILIAN-SPEAK AND USE MARINE-SPEAK ONLY. FOR EXAMPLE:

ONE. YOU ARE NOW ON A 24-HOUR CLOCK. WHEN THE LITTLE HAND IS ON ONE AND THE BIG HAND IS ON TWELVE, IT WILL BE OH-ONE-

HUNDRED. IN THE AFTERNOON IT WILL BE THIRTEEN HUNDRED. IS THAT UNDERSTOOD? REMEMBER: THERE WILL BE A TEST—EVERY SECOND OF EVERY DAY!

TWO. YOUR VOCABULARY HAS CHANGED. FOR EXAMPLE: FLOORS ARE DECKS, DOORS ARE HATCHES, WALLS ARE BULKHEADS, BATHROOMS ARE HEADS, WINDOWS ARE PORTS, STAIRS ARE LADDERS, PANTS ARE TROUSERS, BEDS ARE RACKS AND WRITING PENS ARE INK STICKS.

THREE. WHENEVER A DRILL INSTRUCTOR SAYS 'EARS,' YOU WILL SHOUT 'OPEN!' WHENEVER A DRILL INSTRUCTOR SAYS 'EYEBALLS,' YOU WILL SHOUT 'SNAP!' DO YOU UNDERSTAND ME? I C-A-A-N'T H-E-A-R-R YOU!

SIR, YESSIR! yelled the scared recruits at the top of their lungs.

FOUR. THE CORRIDOR BETWEEN THE RACKS IS THE DRILL INSTRUCTORS' HIGHWAY! IF THEY ARE ON IT, YOU WILL NOT BE ON IT! DO YOU UNDERSTAND ME?

SIR, YESSIR! the recruits shouted.

NEXT! USING THAT MAGIC MARKER, YOU WILL WRITE THE NUMBER 5001 ON YOUR LEFT

HAND. THIS IS YOUR PLATOON NUMBER. YOU ARE NOW A PART OF FIFTH BATTALION, JULIET COMPANY, PLATOON 5001!

NOW! YOU WILL SIGN AND MAIL A COPY OF THIS LETTER TO YOUR FAMILY TELLING THEM YOU HAVE ARRIVED SAFELY AT PARRIS ISLAND, AND YOU WILL WRITE TO THEM REGULARLY. IS THAT CLEAR?

SIR, YESSIR! CLEAR, SIR! replied the anxious recruits.

Pivoting on his heel, the Man in the Hat looked straight at Pepper and shouted, ARE YOU EYE-BALLING ME, RECRUIT PARKER? ARE YOU? DO YOU THINK I'M PRETTY?

"AYE, AYE SIR! SIR, NO—NO SIR!" exclaimed Pepper. "Sir, I'm confused. Is 'I' the same as 'a-y-e,' Sir?"

The drill instructor wasn't expecting a challenge, but he had one! With an explosion that rocked the room, he screamed, I TOLD YOU THERE IS NO 'I!' 'I' IS GONE! JUST LIKE YOU'LL BE IF YOU KEEP ASKING STUPID QUESTIONS! YOU WILL NOW SHOW THE PLATOON HOW TO DO PUSH-UPS! ASSUME THE POSITION! NOW! ONE, LOWER YOUR SKINNY BUTT AN INCH ABOVE THE DECK. TWO, SNAP THAT BODY BACK AND HOLD IT.

THEN DO IT OVER AND OVER AND OVER UNTIL I SAY WHEN! IF YOU QUIT, YOU WILL BE GIVEN TEN MORE! IS THAT CLEAR?

"Aye-aye, Sir," hissed Recruit Parker as he lowered his body toward the floor.

Chapter 5

A HIGH AND TIGHT SURPRISE

After using a magic marker to write platoon number 5001 on his left paw, Pepper followed the other fearful recruits to a place marked BARBER SHOP.

Lurking just inside the door was a sinister-looking man, nearly toothless, wearing a black T-shirt sporting the words LIFE IS GOOD. The barber, holding what looked like a small buzz saw, grinned when he saw the newest batch of recruits. He loved his job. He changed their lives forever in the twenty-five seconds it took for him to shear off their lovely locks. He would be a part of their recurring nightmares right alongside visions of their drill instructor, but for now they belonged entirely to him.

"This is a bad, bad dream," Pepper hissed to the drill instructor. "I don't want a haircut! I just want an apology from the Marine Corps for catnapping me!"

YOUR RECRUITER SAYS OTHERWISE, said the Hat.

"Like I told you, Sir, I don't know any recruiting

sergeant up north! That enlistee would be my cousin Danny, and if he's smart, he's escaped from Parris Island by now!"

SO, RECRUIT, bellowed the drill instructor, YOU'RE CALLING STAFF SERGEANT GOTTAQUOTA IN WESTFIELD, MASSACHUSETTS A LIAR?

"Sir, No Sir!" Pepper responded. "The Staff Sergeant is okay but confused! Like I told you, I'm a five-year-old feline! I can prove I'm not a female! I've never had a haircut, I tell you! Not even a trim! Well, maybe a nice Mohawk like yours would be okay, Your Excellency, Mister Marine, Sir."

NEXT! barked the drill instructor.

Pepper took the paper towel offered by the barber with mixed emotions, asking, "Why does this recruit need a paper towel?"

"Just jump in the chair and find out," coaxed the barber.

"I can jump really high," said Pepper. "In fact, I should jump all the way out the door, and then we wouldn't have this failure to communicate!"

Instead of his usual twenty-five second haircut, it took the barber at least thirty seconds just to figure out where the recruit's haircut should stop. Black and white hair was growing everywhere! "Stop right there, you monster!" growled Pepper. "Just because I have full body hair, there will be NO special poodle cut! Besides, my black and white tuxedo is appropriate for all occasions! Quite frankly, I prefer it to those things the Marines call 'cammies!' They look to me like somebody got carried away with his little brown and green crayons!"

I ORDERED YOU NOT TO TALK! shouted the fearsome Hat. YOU GIRLS WANTED THIS HAIRCUT OR YOU WOULDN'T HAVE ENLISTED. SO JUST SUCK IT UP SO THE MAN CAN DO HIS JOB!

"Sir, I can see your tonsils," hissed Pepper. "And could you tone it down a bit? It's too early in the morning to be caterwauling! What's it take to get a little catnap around here? That nice ledge up there should give me a good view, so I can watch for Danny."

RECRUIT, began the drill instructor in a deadly, hushed tone, YOU BELONG TO THE MARINE CORPS NOW AND WHETHER YOU LIKE IT OR NOT WE WILL MAKE A MARINE OUT OF YOU! YOU MADE YOUR CHOICE WHEN YOU JOINED—SO SHUT UP AND PAY ATTENTION TO WHAT YOU'RE TOLD TO DO!

"Like I told you," the cat continued, "when Jessie

Lee arrives with the Sheriff, you are going to be so-o-o sorry you didn't listen to me!"

Zip, zip and a zap! All of Pepper's luxurious head fur floated down into a black pile on the floor.

DEPOSIT THOSE LOVELY LOCKS OF HAIR IN THE TRASH CAN, WIPE YOURSELF CLEAN WITH YOUR TOWEL AND GET IN THE HALLWAY! NEXT! glowered the drill instructor.

"It's all a big misunderstanding!" cried Pepper. "Honest! Dear Lord, what have I gotten myself into and how do I get out of this mess? There's no 'me' anymore for Cousin Danny or Jessie Lee to look for," Pepper moaned. "This cat looks just like all the other recruits! Well, almost."

In fifty-five seconds a haircut had changed Pepper forever. He no longer recognized himself, and his new plan for survival was to "go along to get along"—at least until he was rescued. Then it would be big time payback!

On the brighter side, now that he looked more like all the other real recruits, maybe he'd have a better chance of slipping away for his rendezvous at Fourth Battalion.

That thought became a memory when the Man in the Hat suddenly appeared, screaming YOU BETTER START SNAPPIN' AND POPPIN' WHEN

I TALK TO YOU! YOU BETTER MOVE LIKE FREAKIN' LIGHTNING, DO YOU UNDERSTAND?

SIR, AYE, AYE, SIR! fifty-one bald recruits screamed in unison.

Chapter 6

A BUCKET FOR HIS HEAD

After the horrific haircut, Pepper and the other recruits knew their perfect little worlds had exploded into complete chaos. Every time they found an exit, it was blocked by the drill instructor from hell! He was everywhere, yelling, screaming, pointing, stomping and acting like he still wasn't glad they were there.

Before the recruits could catch their breath, the Man in the Hat marched them through a supply room where they were issued all the clothes they would wear or need for their thirteen-week incarceration.

"I definitely don't need all that junk!" Pepper exclaimed. "I already told you, Mister Boss Man, I'm a lean, mean, self-cleaning machine! Naturally, there's a hairball that comes up every now and then—but stuff happens! I don't want a Kevlar helmet, ditty bag, rifle towel, utilities, boots, poncho, cartridge belt, socks, shaving stuff or a bucket for my head, Sir! This recruit told you, he is self-sufficient. He doesn't need anything that will slow him down! Besides, I bet I can outrun you! Wanna race?"

FOR THE LAST TIME, screamed the drill instructor, 'I' IS GONE! YOU WILL NEVER, EVER REFER TO YOURSELF AS ME, MYSELF OR I! THOSE WORDS LEFT ON THE BUS THAT BROUGHT YOU HERE! DO YOU UNDERSTAND ME? NOW, RECRUIT PARKER, FOR SMART-MOUTHING ME, ASSUME THE POSITION AND GIVE ME FIVE PUSH-UPS!

"Push-ups? Like, duh, I've done those already," complained the accidental recruit as he assumed the position.

Wearing their new Kevlar helmets and clutching their equipment issue close to their chests, the recruits were then herded to their temporary home. Except for fifty-one unmade beds and two white lines on the floor, the room was empty.

Meticulously, the drill instructor showed the recruits how to make up their racks the military way, the sheets tightly tucked in at each corner with a forty-five degree fold. After that exercise he explained the purpose of the two white lines running the length of the room.

THEY ARE CRITICAL TO YOU, cautioned the Hat, BECAUSE IF YOU ARE NOT STANDING AT THE LINE WITH YOUR TOE ON IT WITHIN THREE SECONDS OF MY COMMAND TO TOE THE

LINE, YOU WILL RECEIVE INCENTIVE TRAINING KNOWN AS QUARTERDECKING! IS THAT CLEAR?

SIR, YES SIR! the ragged recruits shouted. At this point they would have agreed with the devil himself if it meant they wouldn't be punished. But the night had just begun….

With his next breath, the drill instructor yelled, NOW! TOE THE LINE! Fifty-five frazzled recruits scrambled over each other, trying to toe the line in three seconds. Fifteen didn't make it.

Before they headed out for their first meal on Parris Island, the drill instructor taught his new recruits the basic steps of the military dance: CLOSE ORDER DRILL.

Then, with each recruit holding a flashlight and moving with all the finesse of a class of five-year-old ballerinas, they were marched off into the night.

Under silent protest, but to please the Man in the Hat, Pepper joined the group. The tomcat was so confused and so very tired; but he could smell food and he was marching towards it! Was it possible that food still existed on the planet? "Yes," he decided, "there is a God, even if He's leading me to a hall full of messes!"

Later, Pepper used his ink stick to write his first

letter.

Dear Jessie Lee,

Did I tell you they catnapped me? Well, not only that. You won't recognize me with this new haircut. And my new hat is not something I picked up in downtown Beaufort, but it was free and goes with the rest of my new wardrobe, at least for now.

I've already used the one phone call to you that the warden allowed, so for now I'll keep writing until I see you again. Please pray real hard for me and come take me home as soon as possible. PLEASE!

Love, your catnapped son,

Pepper

Chapter 7

THE HALL OF MESSES

"Mister Drill Instructor, Sir," began Recruit Parker, "just so you know, in the cathouse the early morning routine is for Jessie Lee to lovingly brush me and my brother, Bubba Billy, before offering us our choice of morning treats.

"Sir, I know it's a lot to ask," Pepper continued. "but would you please consider extending these niceties to me? Remember, I did say please. It won't take long, and it will help me pass the time until Jessie Lee comes for me."

LOUDER, RECRUIT PARKER, bellowed the drill instructor. I DID NOT HEAR WHAT YOU JUST SAID! WOULD YOU LIKE TO SPEAK UP OR SHUT YOUR FACE?

Quietly, Pepper responded, "I'm talking again? Shut my face? Okay, but when do we eat, Your Holiness? Do they have any Science Diet or IAMS cat food? This recruit especially likes the crunchy crab or shrimp flavor!"

YOU WILL EAT WHATEVER IS PREPARED AT

THE MESS HALL AND YOU WILL LIKE IT! Roared the Hat.

"SIR, NOSSIR, thank you Sir," responded Pepper, "but this recruit doesn't eat anywhere called a mess hall no matter what they're serving! It's always been his policy to cover up any messes he makes. Maybe you could call Pizza Hut for some nice pepperoni pizza—and don't forget the extra cheese."

It had been a long night for the Man in the Hat and this particular recruit was trying his patience. Parker danced rings around the other recruit ballerinas, proclaiming that he wasn't supposed to be there!

AN ACCIDENTAL RECRUIT? INDEED! I JUST NEED TO SHOW HIM WHO'S BOSS, the drill instructor decided. But he was fast running out of options, because if he allowed the recruit to quit this early in the process, he would get a black mark on his record. SUCK IT UP AND POUR ON THE DISCIPLINE, the Hat muttered to himself. THIS WAS THE MANTRA OF HIS MARINE CORPS—AND IT WORKED!

Although he complained, food was now paramount in Pepper's thoughts. He needed food soon or he would collapse.

LISTEN UP, GIRLS, directed the drill instructor. WHEN WE ENTER THE MESS HALL, YOU WILL

NOT RUN YOUR MOUTHS, UNDERSTOOD? YOU HAVE ELEVEN MINUTES TO EAT YOUR FOOD AND I'D BETTER NOT FIND ANY TAKE-OUTS ON YOU WHEN WE LEAVE! DO YOU UNDERSTAND ME?

SIR, YES SIR the hungry recruits replied.

"Well," thought Pepper, "I always did tend to eat fast, but this is ridiculous! I have to swallow stuff I don't like or recognize, and my eleven minutes are ticking away fast." Tick—chomp—tock— swallow—tick—chomp—tock—swallow. Tick-tock-tick-tock-tick-tock went the clock.

As the new arrivals gulped their meal, another platoon of recruits entered the mess hall. Unlike Pepper's platoon, these recruits were stomping, swaggering and executing pivots and turns like he'd seen on television. Then, to his dismay, they stepped up to a special buffet filled with steak, eggs and potatoes! And not only that! It was an "all you can eat" buffet!

"Why are all those recruits stomping around with so much attitude?" Pepper asked his drill instructor. "I thought we were supposed to be quiet. Don't they know being rowdy at the table is rude here in the low country? And, while you're at it, Mister Marine, would you mind asking the chef to bring out some of that special grub for us too?"

THEY'RE ENTITLED, the Hat explained. THAT PLATOON JUST FINISHED THE CRUCIBLE, AND THEY GRADUATE NEXT WEEK.

"My favorite thing!" exclaimed Pepper. "Tell them I'll be there to cheer them on. You see, I really did plan to attend recruit graduation—just like I do every Friday morning. That's why I was at Recruit Receiving. I was just early for graduation. You see? I'm not who you think I am!"

Later the drill instructor reflected on the new batch of recruits. Some were good, some mediocre and some just plain pitiful. And then there was Recruit Parker! He took the cake!

In all his fifteen years in the Marine Corps, he had never seen such a recruit! "There's something different about the recruit's ears," he mused. "NO, a LOT different! Is it my imagination or were they on top of his head? That recruit also has a problem keeping his cover off his yellow eyes, but so do a few other recruits. A touch of glue helps, but their ears aren't on top of their heads! And not only that," he thought. "Recruit Parker's feet are so small the Supply Sergeant had to trade favors to get a smaller pair of boots from the women at Fourth Battalion. But that little rascal has endless energy and really tries hard to keep up with the rest of the platoon even while complaining that he isn't supposed to be here. He has HEART—and that's what matters most in a recruit," smiled the Man in the Hat. He would watch and wait, giving Recruit Parker a break now and then—but that was all he would give. The recruit had to rise to the high water mark just like all the others who had gone before him.

Moments later, the drill instructor caught his breath and cringed—DID I JUST SAY THAT RECRUIT HAD YELLOW EYES?

CATNIP

Chapter 8

A MOMENT OF TRUTH

After allowing the recruits a moment to settle down, the Man in the Hat shouted, LISTEN UP! DO YOU RECRUITS KNOW THE MARINE CORPS' POSITION ON ILLEGAL DRUGS? Several hands shot into the air, but most remained tightly closed at their sides.

IN CASE THERE'S ANY DOUBT WHATSOEVER IN YOUR LITTLE PEA BRAINS, the drill instructor snarled, I'M GOING TO TELL YOU! THE MARINE CORPS DOES NOT TOLERATE DRUG USE!

While scanning the faces of the group of terrified recruits for their reaction, the drill instructor thought he detected movement on Recruit Parker although he didn't appear to be moving. Wait, was that something waving to him from Recruit Parker's skivvies? Too big for an Irish pennant. Suddenly, the drill instructor turned livid. In a flash he snatched the guilty "thread" that was attached to Mister Mouse, who was enjoying Pepper's leftover catnip inside his secret pocket! Without the mouse's tail to wedge it open, Pepper's secret pocket disappeared from view.

WHAT'S THIS? the drill instructor bellowed as he held the mouse up by the tail. LUNCH? LOOKS LIKE TEN PUSH-UPS TO ME!

"Now wait just a cotton-picking minute," demanded the little recruit. That mouse is not illegal! I caught him all legit! And that catnip is for medicinal purposes!"

SAVE IT FOR YOUR MOMENT OF TRUTH, RECRUIT! I'LL JUST TAKE MISTER MOUSE OUTSIDE WHERE HE CAN PLAY.

"Mister Marine," wailed Pepper, "I really don't want a Moment of Truth! The only things I've ever done that were illegal were accidents!"

HAVE YOU EVER BEEN ARRESTED OR SERVED TIME IN JAIL, RECRUIT? asked the drill instructor.

"I have nothing to confess, and no, I don't have a police record," Pepper replied. "Although there was that time me and my brother, Bubba Billy ran out of ice cream, and we borrowed some from the Piggly Wiggly grocery store—but nobody got hurt! Just whip out the waiver for me, Mister Hat, and the others can get on with show and tell. Just remember, I'm only a spectator—just passing through. That's my story, and I'm sticking with it, so don't bother asking me again!"

RECRUIT, THAT IS THE STUPIDEST EXCUSE I'VE EVER HEARD, seethed the drill instructor. SHUT YOUR MOUTH AND GET YOUR SORRY BUTT OVER TO THE CHIN-UP BAR AND GIVE ME FIVE! NOW!

"But, how can this recruit meow the truth to you if he keeps his meower shut?" asked Pepper as he quickly reached for the bar.

"Lord of the Cats," begged Pepper, "please hear my prayer and feel my pain! What have I gotten myself into? And how do I get out of this mess? H-E-L-L-P!"

Z Z Z

Chapter 9

SLEEP, WONDERFUL SLEEP

After the big faux paw over at Recruit Receiving and seventeen hours of sheer madness, Recruit Parker was finally allowed to relax on the top bunk of his new home. His bunkmate, Recruit Skippy, from Amelia Island, had reminded his new friend how to make up his rack with the sheet corners tucked in just right. Recruit Skippy wanted to be a Marine Aviator.

Finally, after the required bedtime ritual of thanking God for blessing His Marine Corps and shouting, HONOR, COURAGE, COMMITMENT—MARINE CORPS! the exhausted recruits climbed into bed and lay stiffly at attention. Recruit Parker made one gigantic leap onto the top bunk, climbed under the sheet and immediately released his whiskers and tail from their protective sheaths. He calmed himself by silently licking his magnificent coat of black and white fur to perfection. Finally, when his heart stopped racing, he closed his eyes. Curling into a furry ball, Pepper mentally called out to God, Jessie Lee and Bubba for rescue, while his mind drifted into another world where cats ruled and catnip was free.

As Pepper slept, invisible hands gently tucked the sheets around his exhausted body. A whispered lullaby filled his ears, and he was surrounded in lovely white light. The tomcat dreamed of his Mistress, Jessie Lee, and his favorite place in the sun while Madam MoJoe stood guard.

Chapter 10

A DIFFERENT KIND OF DEPOSIT

TOE THE LINE! GET ON LINE NOW! GET! ON! LINE! NOW! screamed the drill instructor.

Pepper leapt onto the white line and then followed the other recruits to the head for the required pee sample. He tried to imitate the others and did his best to fill the little cup. But it wasn't easy, and his attempt to cover it up afterward just made the Hat more livid—as if that was possible.

"Could it be that the drill instructor's mother was agitated when he was born?" Pepper wondered. "Maybe that was the problem; or he never got a lesson in how to mind his manners. Anything is possible," he thought, "but the drill instructor was angry about everything and with everybody in sight, reminding them they were not at home! Like they needed to be reminded," he snickered.

WIPE THAT GRIN OFF YOUR FACE, RECRUIT PARKER! warned the Hat. LAUGHS AND SMILES ARE NASTIES AND WILL NOT BE TOLERATED!

NOW, the frowning drill instructor shouted, YOU

WILL MARCH IN FORMATION, BEGINNING ALWAYS WITH YOUR LEFT FOOT. HERE WE GO, AH LEFT FOOT, YOUR LEFT, AH LEFT FOOT, YOUR LEFT....

The recruits' feet soon took them to a place where M-16 rifles were issued to them. Now that their rifle was to be a constant companion, they would learn to love it, clean it, take it on marches, carry it to the mess hall and, at the end of the day, hang it on the ends of their racks.

"No bullets! Drat!" exclaimed Pepper to himself.

"Sir, this recruit is ready to retreat, Mister Spit 'n Shine Marine! You win! This recruit admits to being a non-hacker and guilty of failure to adapt to the Marine Corps way of life!"

JUST FOR THAT LITTLE SPEECH, RECRUIT PARKER, GIVE ME FIVE SIT-UPS! NO, GIVE ME FIVE AND FIVE MORE FOR SERGEANT BLISTER!

Chapter 11

THE M-16 MEETS MR. VELCRO

"Sir," began the accidental recruit, "this is getting to be ver-r-ry in-ter-est-ing. Exactly what part of this recruit would be considered shoulders? Do they come with the rifle? Maybe this recruit could just wear that nice towel with the outline of the rifle on his shoulder!"

RECRUIT, YOU ARE TOO WEIRD TO BE IN MY MARINE CORPS, the drill instructor sneered. FIGURE IT OUT! AND WHILE YOU'RE AT IT, HERE'S A BIG ROLL OF VELCRO!

"Sir, Yessir! Thank you Sir," the big cat purred. If you insist, Velcro it is! Lots and lots of Velcro!" agreed Pepper. "This recruit is all zipped up and falling into line. Picking himself up has always been a piece of cake, Sir! This recruit will just quickly lick himself and pretend he wanted to fall. It's a well-known feline secret, don't you know?"

PARKER! shouted the drill instructor. IF YOU GET ANY SHORTER I MIGHT LOSE YOU IN ALL THAT EQUIPMENT! ARE YOU SURE YOU'RE NOT

A FEMALE RECRUIT? STRAIGHTEN UP AND LISTEN LOUD!

"Sir, this recruit is not short, Sir! He is very large for a feline, Sir, and he's getting larger every minute! Remember, all cats are felines. Sir, Nosir, this recruit is not feminine but he is a feline! Wanna see?" The Hat declined.

"Just so you'll know the difference," Pepper added, you'll find my canine pal Hummer over at the Visitors' Center—you do know what a canine is, don't you, Sir?"

THAT YANKEE RECRUITER MUST HAVE BEEN PICKING HIS NOSE WHEN HE FOUND YOU, RECRUIT PARKER! roared the Hat. YOU WILL REMEMBER THAT YOU ARE IN MY TERRITORY! YOU ARE NOT AT HOME! YOU ARE NOT BACK ON THE BLOCK! EVERYTHING YOU DO WILL BE DONE QUICKLY AND LOUDLY! DO YOU UNDERSTAND ME! MOVE IT! MOVE IT! NOW!

"Sir, Nosir, this recruit never met a recruiter before, Sir. But if you say they need to meet their quotas or else, I won't argue. The real truth is that this recruit's paw prints on the enlistment papers were forged! SIR! THIS RECRUIT HAS BEEN CATNAPPED! Besides, he doesn't need these cammies because, like I told you, Sir, he wears his black and white tux at all times!"

NOT ON MY WATCH YOU DON'T! the drill instructor retorted. AND YOU WILL NEVER REFER TO A DRILL INSTRUCTOR AS "YOU!"

"Okay, Sir," Pepper stated in his best authoritative voice. "We've established that Parris Island is your territory. I don't want it—you can have it."

Stunned by the mouthy recruit, the drill instructor's eyes bulged. I? I? Red-faced, he screamed: I IS GONE! GONE! SHUT YOUR MOUTH, RECRUIT PARKER! UNDERSTAND? NOT ONE MORE WORD! EVERYONE OUTSIDE—NOW!

SIR, AYE, SIR! screamed the recruits in return.

Pepper joined the rest of the recruits who had hurried down the ladder to their place in front of the barracks. The Hat then led the pitiful bunch of recruits onto the parade field, where they were drilled until they felt they couldn't drill anymore. And then they REALLY started drill time.

AH LEFT, LEFT, LEFT RIGHT—YOUR LEFT, chanted the Hat. While there was some improvement in the platoon as a whole, several of the smallest recruits were finding it hard to execute the required thirty-inch step.

"Sir," shouted Recruit Parker, "this recruit is trying

to keep in step, but you need to remember he has two left feet! He also has two right feet!"

JUST PUT ONE FOOT IN FRONT OF THE OTHER AND WE'LL ALL GET TO WHERE WE'RE GOING, ordered the Hat. YOU DO WANT TO GET TO WHERE WE'RE GOING, DON'T YOU? RECRUIT PARKER!

"Sir, this recruit does not know where we're going, and if it's all the same to the drill instructor, he would rather not go. He'll just sit in that big oak tree over there and wait for you to come back."

With that declaration, the cat jumped onto the tree trunk and climbed to the top before the drill instructor could blink. The Hat in charge called a halt to the platoon while he ran back to where he thought the recruit had disappeared. The limbs of the massive oak tree dripped with gray Spanish moss, and its branches of green leaves gave the recruit a perfect hiding place.

RECRUIT PARKER, YOU'D BETTER GET DOWN HERE THIS MINUTE, shrieked the drill instructor. DON'T MAKE ME HAVE TO COME UP THERE AFTER YOU! YOU'RE IN ENOUGH TROUBLE ALREADY, SO YOU'D BETTER DO AS YOU'RE TOLD—AND DO IT NOW! YOU HAVE UNTIL THE COUNT OF THREE!

Those words struck fear in the little recruit's heart! Jessie Lee used those exact words whenever she had reached her absolute limit of patience with him or his brother. At that point it was always easier to just give up and take the punishment rather than prolong the inevitable. He had never chosen to find out what came after her "three," and he sure didn't want to find out what came after the drill instructor's "three!"

ONE, the Hat began. Before TWO became a word, the little recruit had jumped from the tree and landed on his feet in front of the fuming Hat.

WHEN WE GET BACK TO THE SQUAD BAY, the frustrated Hat told Pepper, I'LL FILE A REPORT OF THIS INCIDENT! YOU'LL HAVE TO ANSWER TO A HIGHER AUTHORITY, AND WE'LL JUST SEE WHAT THEY HAVE TO SAY ABOUT THIS LITTLE ESCAPADE OF YOURS! NOW GET YOUR SORRY SELF BACK WITH YOUR PLATOON.

"My bad, but hey, I can do this," hissed Pepper as he caught step with the other recruits. "With the help of Mister Velcro, I'll just have to show these boys how an alpha cat gets the job done. I bet if I serenade the Hat with a song, he may forget about that little escapade," the accidental recruit concluded. "Nothing could be finer than to be in Car-o-li-na in the mor-r-ning," sang Pepper—as loudly as possible. He couldn't remember what line came next, but it didn't matter, because the Man in the Hat was already headed his way.

Chapter 12

PEARLY WHITES ON PARADE

"Whadda ya think, Doc?" Pepper asked the Navy dentist. "Nice weapons, don't you agree? Have you ever seen such beautiful canines in your life? They're honed to a point that equals any sword in the Corps! I'm a lean, mean, fightin' machine, Sir! No cavities and no flossing necessary, Mister Dentist. Just make sure the chow in the mess hall includes lots of hard nuggets for that polished effect."

The dentist was pleased with the healthy teeth the recruit displayed, although he was concerned and puzzled about the two pointed top teeth in the front that overlapped his bottom lip.

"Now wait just a cotton-picking minute!" the accidental recruit exclaimed. Cats are supposed to have pointy teeth! And those canine teeth are not dog types! Don't you know anything? Maybe you'd like to see my personal bayonets? There are eighteen in all, conveniently attached to my paws and entirely retractable. Not impressed? How about giving me an On the Grass Pass, and this recruit will just take this opportunity to mosey on out of here."

GOING SOMEWHERE RECRUIT PARKER? YOU'D BETTER GET IN LINE! threatened the now familiar voice of the Man in the Hat.

"Oh, hello, Mister Drill Instructor! This recruit was just looking for you!" Pepper said as he ran toward the line of recruits.

Chapter 13

LOOKING FOR JESSIE LEE

Pepper kept watching the parking lot for the Catmobile, knowing it was only a matter of time before Jessie Lee, Bubba Billy and his faithful Pet Pals rescued him from this bad dream. But until they showed up, he figured another letter to Jessie Lee could work as a backup, and it would make his drill instructor happy if he wrote that required letter home.

D-I-S-C-I-P-L-I-N-E

Dear Jessie Lee,

I have a teeny-weeny problem: like HELP! At your earliest convenience, would you mind coming over to Parris Island and explain things to the hired help? I'll admit that I shouldn't have been out of the house last night, but I promised Cousin Danny I'd meet him at Recruit Receiving. He wasn't there, and now they think I'm him!

In just the last fifteen hours they've catnapped me, shaved my head, taken my mouse, dressed me in a butt ugly uniform and changed my name to a number! I know that's hard to believe, but these guards don't know how to take NO for an answer.

I'm begging you, Sweet Mama! Call the Sheriff! A crime has been committed! Oops, that won't work! I'm told Mister Uniform Code of Military Justice owns me now! Just call Big Bill at the AMVETS to come with you, and you won't have to shoot anybody. But hurry, I'm sinking fast!

Love, Pepper

AMVETS
POST 70
(Happy Hideaway)

Chapter 14

MAYDAY!! MAYDAY!!

Pepper's MAYDAY call from Recruit Receiving was the talk of his Beaufort territory. Their leader, Alpha Cat Pepper, was in deep, serious trouble, and the Pet Pals had to do whatever was necessary to help him!

Pepper's cat brother, Bubba Billy, had listened to P-2's* message on the answering machine and erased it before Jessie Lee heard it, for Bubba knew she would rush off to the base and pitch one of her infamous hissy-fits right in front of the Commanding General. He had also taken care of P-2's latest letter to Jessie Lee, because there was still no need to upset her.

Taking command of the situation, Bubba called an emergency meeting of the Pet Pals. The assortment of animals that hung out, hunted and played together quickly arrived at their secret clubhouse, the Happy Hideaway.

**P-2: Bubba's nickname for his brother, Pepper Parker.*

The clubhouse where the Pet Pals had their meetings was located behind American Veterans (AMVETS) Post 70 in Port Royal. Today the Post's chef was Big Bill, one of their favorites, because he often saved some of the kitchen's leftovers for them. This was one of those nights, and Bill's bloodhound, Marvin, made the delivery of savory hamburgers and French fries.

The fact that P-2 had gotten himself into yet another big-time mess was just another crisis Bubba had to handle when he'd rather be snoozing in the sunshine. But rescuing his big brother was his duty. Plus, it looked like it would be an adventure he would enjoy.

The best part of the whole affair, thought Bubba Billy, was that after he rescued P-2, the clan would naturally promote him to the status of alpha cat. Pepper would have to take orders from him, and what a glorious day that would be.

Bubba admitted that taking on the United States Marine Corps was not something to be taken lightly, but it was, in his mind, doable—with a little help from his friends.

The group assembled in the Happy Hideaway and discussed several plans of attack. While they were busy, Bubba's thoughts drifted past the rescue to how the club members would greet him and P-2 back home with loud cheers and a celebration. Later, he would take P-2 home to their mistress, where he would enjoy a good old-fashioned Come to Jessie Lee moment. P-2 would have to confess and ask forgiveness for going out without permission, and his punishment would naturally fit the crime. Bubba thought for sure that if Pepper's disappearance had broken their mistress's heart, she would be thrilled to have him back; but given the circumstances, he figured P-2 wouldn't be allowed out of the house for at least a month. That would give him plenty of time to assert himself and claim the status of territorial alpha cat, replacing his big brother. P-2 had made a humongous mistake, and Bubba was going to milk it for all it was worth.

5
10
15
20

Chapter 15

GOOD MORNING, SLEEPYHEADS!

The bright overhead lights, accompanied by the screams of the drill instructor, again caught Pepper by surprise, but he quickly landed on the floor with a thump. Rubbing his eyes to clear the sleep away, he tried to reorient himself. Exactly where was this place? Surely he wasn't waking up from a party, because his body ached all over, and he was surrounded by humans—all male. "There's something terribly wrong with this picture," Pepper thought.

All the air and space in the squad bay seemed to be sucked up by the drill instructor shouting his loud, repetitive order for the recruits to TOE THE LINE! But, no matter how fast they moved, it wasn't fast enough. MOVE! FASTER! NOW! ANY DAY, LADIES! OH, I'LL WAIT FOR YOU! the Hat bellowed.

Pepper reacted quickly and was on line in front of his rack when the drill instructor stalked past him on the Drill Instructors' Highway.

Last night he had finally drifted off to sleep, and

the morning had come much too quickly. He was in a living nightmare, but to survive the moment, he accepted the fact that he would have to play along until the inevitable happened. Either Jessie Lee or the Pet Pals would come for him. “Maybe today is the big day,” he thought, hopefully.

Because quitting wasn’t in the big cat’s vocabulary, he would just suck it up and deal with whatever they threw at him—at least for now. He was still an accidental Marine recruit, and there were probably worse places he could be—like the animal shelter on death row!

After a twenty-minute visit to the head, the recruits were ordered to sweep the barracks’ deck with hand brushes. This wasn’t Pepper’s idea of a nice way to start the day, and it was an insult to his earned position of alpha cat as well. At home Jessie Lee did all the cleaning. Naturally, he covered up whatever he deposited in the sandbox, but he didn’t mind helping out.

Unfortunately, that morning the large letters on the wall still spelled D-I-S-C-I-P-L-I-N-E, a reminder of where he was and the fact that he was going to have to stay there—at least until the brothers from the Pet Pals showed up. It wasn’t a matter of if but when they would rescue him.

After chow, Pepper and Recruit Skippy were ordered to scrub the deck of the squad bay—with toothbrushes! The big cat tried to find comfort in the fact that with a little help from Jessie Lee, his Pet Pals and his brother; he would soon be out of this psycho ward. He tried to keep positive thoughts about all the wonderful things he would do when freedom reigned; a parade down Bay Street with the Marine Band playing especially for him on a day designated by the mayor of Beaufort to welcome him home—PEPPER DAY. A nice assortment of refreshments and possibly a medal awarded to him before the gang later gathered in the Happy Hideaway to write his legacy....

RECRUIT PARKER! came a familiar shout. YOU'RE WEARING A HOLE IN THAT ONE INCH SQUARE OF DECK SPACE. GET YOUR MIND OFF OTHER THINGS AND PAY ATTENTION TO DUTY, counseled the Hat.

Turning to the entire platoon, the drill instructor shouted, WHAT IS THE MEANING OF DISCIPLINE?

Pepper joined his fellow recruits in shouting, SIR, DISCIPLINE IS THE INSTANT WILLING OBEDIENCE TO ALL ORDERS, RESPECT FOR AUTHORITY, SELF-RELIANCE AND TEAMWORK, SIR!

Pepper continued to keep a hopeful watch for the Catmobile.

Seated on his footlocker in the squad bay, a downcast Pepper wrote:

Dear Jessie Lee,

Where are you? Please call the General, because I can't take this anymore! I want to go home! Did I tell you they took my mouse? If you could find it in your heart to come for me, I promise never, ever to wander off again after you've gone to bed. I miss you so much, and I'm not sure how much longer I can hold out. Love, your catnapped son,

*Pepper**

**Bubba read this, Pepper's latest letter, and hid it in a safe place, away from Jessie Lee's sharp eyes.*

Chapter 16

MEET YOUR NEW BEST NIGHTMARE

At Oh-Dark-Thirty, to wake the recruits, the glowering drill instructor flipped on the overhead lights and shouted, TOE THE LINE – NOW! Banging a trashcan with a stick, he sent the lid flying off the walls like a Frisbee out of control, yelling, NOW! GET YOUR SORRY HIDES ON LINE NOW! MOVE IT! FASTER! NOW! WAKE UP, LADIES!

Once again, the sudden brightness and loud noise revealed fifty-one terrified males, most of them still half asleep, leaping out of their racks, running into each other or falling down, scrambling to toe the line.

"But it's Saturday morning," Pepper complained. "Fruit Loops and cartoon time! Where's the TV?"

YOU ARE NOT AT HOME, RECRUITS, explained the screaming Hat! ON THE LINE! NOW! DON'T MAKE ME COME OVER THERE! RISE AND SHINE! MOVE IT! NOW!

The recruits were allowed twenty minutes to

shower, shave and do whatever else they could push and shove their way into and out of in the allotted time. There were always too many arms and legs and never enough time. The tall ones always took the lead, leaving the smaller ones to do the best they could with the minutes left.

Miraculously, after exactly twenty minutes, they were all dressed and on line, ready for whatever the drill instructors had conjured up for them to do next. If they had known, ninety-five percent of the platoon would probably have made a run for the main gate.

Unknown to the recruits, but right on schedule, the day called Pick-Up had arrived. The recruits were ordered to pack up all their gear and take it with them to their new home, an empty squad bay on the second floor of Building #5000, Parris Island Recruit Training Depot, Parris Island, SC 29905.

As they dutifully marched into the early morning, Pepper whispered to Recruit Skippy, who was marching next to him, "I heard the drill instructors talking about a 'pick-up party!' Do you think maybe it's one where we'll have treats and meet some nice girls? Maybe one will pick me up. My tuxedo is shiny clean. Do you think the girls will be from town or the Fourth Battalion? I missed a party there last night. Do you think it's like a play date?" Pepper was getting more and more excited as he ran the different scenarios through his mind. Recruit Skippy didn't answer. The recruits were marching to a pick-up party all right—one called BLACK SATURDAY.

To keep the new recruits in a high state of anxiety, the Hats never told them what would come next. The recruits just knew that whatever their drill instructors told them to do, they had better do it, faster and louder than it had ever been done before.

On this particular morning the recruits thought they had already been dragged through a knothole backwards and stomped on, but today's festivities would mark the beginning of their REAL recruit training. They didn't know it, but based on what was waiting for them today, everything they had encountered up to this point had been child's play.

Chapter 17

SHOW TIME!

After they arrived at their permanent home and had stowed their gear in the green footlockers they found under their new racks, the recruits sat cross-legged on the concrete floor in front of a closed door.

The small room adjacent to the door to the squad bay was called the drill instructors' "House." It contained a bunk, a desk, two chairs, a small bathroom and a closet complete with an iron and ironing board to refresh the sharp uniform creases. The Senior Drill Instructor would use the desk on which to track each recruit's test results, performance, weight and offenses. Located at the end of the room was the all-important one-way mirror focused on the recruits in the squad bay.

With mixed emotions, the platoon's team of drill instructors stood looking out at their charges through the mirror. Staff Sergeant Awesome, the Senior Drill Instructor, laughed out loud as he thought of all the hard work that lay ahead of him. BEING A DRILL INSTRUCTOR ISN'T A JOB, he reflected, IT'S A

WAY OF LIFE! And he absolutely loved it!

Like most drill instructors, the Staff Sergeant's job played havoc with his family life, but his wife, Gale, and the kids loved him and kept the home fires burning while he "made Marines."

Last week the four of them had gathered at the dining room table to review their schedules on the calendar. First, Staff Sergeant Awesome highlighted the coming Saturday, the day he would pick up his next recruit platoon. Second, he showed his young son, Jack, how to use a red crayon to draw a big smiley face on the day of the recruits' graduation. The two months in between would be chaotic for all of them, but they were a winning team and had gone through this ordeal before. Gale worked part-time as the base librarian but shared child-care duties with the other military wives. They had formed a "Band of Mothers" who car-pooled and supported one another while their husbands were busy doing Marine things. Although they lived on base, sometimes it seemed as though their husbands were on another planet.

As the Senior squared the dark brown campaign hat onto his shaved head, he checked his uniform in the mirror and smiled. Absolute Marine Corps perfection! Time to get this show on the road!

While the drill instructors kept out of sight, the Juliet

Company Commander, Captain Boucoup, stepped through the door to greet the recruits who had immediately jumped to their feet. On the shoulders of his Class A uniform he wore silver railroad tracks, depicting his rank as captain. He also wore several rows of brightly colored personal and campaign ribbons on his chest that had been awarded to him for his service in Iraq.

Before beginning his welcome speech, Captain Boucoup paused, mentally evaluating the recruits who were now squatting in front of him. "Not the best we've had this year," he mused. "But my Drill Instructors are the best in the business, and they won't stop until these recruits are given every possible chance to become Marines."

Briefly, he told the recruits that he spoke for the Commanding General when he welcomed them to the Marine Corps Recruit Depot. He made it sound like a wonderful place for them to be, but assured them that "The training here is tough, and we will accept nothing less than the very best effort from each of you. It is my drill instructors' duty to make sure that every attempt will be made to provide each of you with excellent training." He turned and stepped to the right side of the entry.

Replacing the Company Commander, First Lieutenant Chevron, the Series Commander, strode to center stage wearing a single silver bar on each shoulder of his uniform. His voice sounded unsympathetic when he addressed the seated recruits, warning, "There's only one way on and one way off this island—and that's the causeway. Trying to swim away will only make the sharks happy, and your bag of bones will be a long time reaching shore, if it makes it at all. Your drill instructors are among the finest Marines in the Marine Corps, and you WILL follow their orders without question. If you have any concerns they can't handle, access the chain of command through the Series Drill Instructor." That said, the Lieutenant turned and stepped to the left of the door.

The busy door swung open again, and into the vacated space stepped a tall, muscled Marine dressed in utilities. He wore a dark brown campaign hat and, at his narrow waist, a shiny black belt— the emblem of the Senior Drill Instructor. Following him into the room were two additional drill instructors who took an at ease position on either side of him. Stone-faced, the Senior took a moment to look into the eyes of the recruits sitting on the floor in front of him. First, he introduced himself as Staff Sergeant Awesome, the Platoon's Senior Drill Instructor. He then introduced his assistants, Second Hat, Sergeant Skittles and Third Hat, Sergeant Clifton.

Following the introductions, Staff Sergeant Awesome gave the recruits assurances that everything that could be done would be done to get them through training. Speaking to them as a father might, he told them he had only their best interests at heart, and they could tell him anything and everything. He continued, I AM NOT GOING TO THREATEN YOU WITH PHYSICAL HARM, ABUSE YOU OR HARASS YOU. NOR WILL I TOLERATE SUCH BEHAVIOR FROM ANYONE ELSE—MARINE OR RECRUIT. IF ANYONE SHOULD ABUSE OR MISTREAT YOU, I WILL EXPECT YOU TO REPORT SUCH INCIDENTS TO ME. FURTHERMORE, IF YOU BELIEVE THAT I HAVE MISTREATED YOU, I EXPECT YOU TO REPORT IT TO THE SERIES COMMANDER.

Pepper's eyes moistened at the gentle words. There was hope for him and the other recruits now that Staff Sergeant Awesome was on their side. He decided that he would pay him a visit and tell him the terrible story about how he had been caught up in this horrible nightmare and was only an accidental recruit. Somebody had to be guilty of something, and it sure wasn't him. He would even go so far as agree not to press charges!

After the Senior finished his speech, the three drill instructors were given "The Drill Instructors' Pledge" by the Company Commander.

THESE RECRUITS ARE ENTRUSTED TO MY CARE.

I WILL TRAIN THEM TO THE BEST OF MY ABILITY.

I WILL DEVELOP THEM INTO SMARTLY DISCIPLINED, PHYSICALLY FIT, BASICALLY TRAINED MARINES, THOROUGHLY INDOCTRINATED IN LOVE OF CORPS AND COUNTRY.

I WILL DEMAND OF THEM, AND DEMONSTRATE BY MY OWN EXAMPLE, THE HIGHEST STANDARDS OF PERSONAL CONDUCT, MORALITY, AND PROFESSIONAL SKILL.

After the oath was taken, the Captain turned the program over to the drill instructors, and the two officers left the area.

Pepper had listened carefully to Staff Sergeant Awesome's promises. Like a light bulb going off, the answer came to him. His Miranda Rights! They hadn't read him his Miranda Rights! Now they had to let him go, because it always happened that way on television! But before Pepper could follow through on his planned release, the nightmare began in earnest.

Sergeant Skittles, the platoon's "Heavy Hat" drill instructor, took center stage. Although short in stature compared to the six-foot tall Senior, he immediately appeared to grow in size right before their eyes! His neatly creased military shirt bulged with muscles, and within seconds, he began to look like the Incredible Hulk as he cited his list of demands.

First, he advised the recruits, IN MY MARINE CORPS DISCIPLINE IS FIRST AND FOREMOST! The recruits didn't remember what came second, because they were then being attacked by what seemed like nine hundred angry drill instructors. They appeared out of nowhere and joined the three platoon drill instructors, swarming, yelling, screaming, pointing and spitting out buckets of rage and sarcasm at the pitiful recruits, instructing them to BACK UP, BACK UP, BACK UP! OH, TAKE YOUR OWN SWEET TIME! ANY DAY! OH, WE'LL WAIT FOR YOU! MOVE IT! MOVE IT, MOVE IT! NOW!!! BACK UP!

To the recruits, the drill instructors were out-of-control, raving maniacs. Red-faced angry, with flying fingers and grotesque features, shouting, raising a booted foot and stamping it on the floor, stabbing their fingers in the recruits' faces and screaming words that made no sense, like PUT ON YOUR LEFT SOCK! TAKE IT OFF AND PUT ON YOUR LEFT SOCK! Issuing multiple orders to the recruits in disorienting sequence, then snarling, ANY DAY NOW! ANY DAY! OH, WE'LL WAIT FOR YOU! BACK UP! BACK UP! I SAID TO BACK UP!

Like a pack of wild animals, the insane drill instructors attacked the recruits' neatly arranged footlockers, flipping them upside down and scattering their belongings everywhere while at the same time accusing them of being messy and lazy. The madmen never stopped moving; they seemed to be everywhere at once.

Huddled under the nearest rack, the accidental recruit instinctively put as much distance as possible between him and his attackers, but he couldn't hide. A drill instructor reached in, dragged him out and pushed his face up so close that Pepper could see all the way down his throat to the mystery meat he'd eaten for breakfast!

ARE YOU HIDING FROM ME RECRUIT? cried the outraged drill instructor. Without thinking, Pepper went into fight or flight mode. Since flight mode wasn't possible, it was the fight response that pumped massive amounts of adrenaline through his system. The cat had unsheathed all eighteen claws earlier, but the drill instructors hadn't even noticed. They were too busy sorting out footlocker gear with spit flying everywhere, veins popping, shouting, MOVE IT! NOW! MOVE IT! ANY DAY! TAKE YOUR OWN SWEET TIME! FASTER! OH, WE'LL WAIT FOR YOU! They lied.

Like all the recruits who weren't accidental, Pepper felt disoriented and mentally begged God to take him on to heaven, because he had just landed in big time hell or, as the old salts called it, BLACK SATURDAY! That didn't begin to cover the level of chaos going on in the squad bay this morning! "If this is Black Saturday, surely there'll be a White Sunday for us to rest!" moaned Pepper.

But Sunday brought only one extra hour of sleep, and the torture began again. An even more hectic schedule began on Monday when the dutiful Hats began to pack thirty hours of activity into a scrawny twenty-four hour day. But the drill instructors were in control and would get the job done according to the Marine Corps Standard Operating Procedure.

Years later, Pepper would remember how, in spite of the drill instructors' ungentlemanly conduct, when the attack ended, each one still looked as though he'd just arrived at church with his razor sharp uniform creases. "Alpha cats never sweat even when they're creating a fine mess of mayhem," he admitted, with a respectful smile.

In yet another hopeful letter home, Pepper wrote:

Dear Jessie Lee,

Today we met our new drill instructors. This recruit is ashamed that he hid under the rack, and they had to drag him out. But, just so you know, they did NOT mind their manners, play nice, or clean up after themselves like you taught me and Bubba to do! After the number the drill instructors pulled in rearranging our footlockers, it will probably take until next Christmas for us recruits to get our gear sorted out. I still can't find my left sock.

Please write as soon as you get this letter. I look for you everywhere, Jessie Lee. This recruit thought he saw Bubba and Fluffy all cozied up under the water truck near the parade field, but I don't think they were looking for me.

Love, Pepper

CHAPTER 18

WHO WAS THAT WEIRD RECRUIT?

Staff Sergeant Awesome beamed as he watched the frazzled recruits try to make sense of Black Saturday. Second Hat Sergeant Skittles and Third Hat Sergeant Clifton, along with the extra Drill Instructors, had created chaos in a short amount of time. It was a reality check to see if the recruits could handle it, a way of sorting out the hackers from the non-hackers. The Hats absolutely loved doing it. Senior Drill Instructor Staff Sergeant Awesome and his assistants would scrape up the shredded recruits and begin the task of building them into "A Few Good Men."

Blinking back an unauthorized tear, the Senior Drill Instructor vowed that no Marine's ghost would ever say, "If only my training had been good enough." No matter what the recruiters send us, he reflected, it's our job to sort them out and make Marines!

Earlier in the day, five non-hackers had been given $25.00 each and a bus ticket home. Two recruits had been sent to the Pork Chop Platoon where they would either lose the excess fat or follow the other five non-hackers and be sent home.

And then there was their accidental recruit. It was hard not to take special notice of the strange youngster with an abundance of black hair and yellow eyes. He didn't jump when the drill instructors blasted him; he just stood at attention, listened to instructions and tried his best to do exactly what was commanded—as though he was on fire! Staff Sergeant Awesome had never seen anyone quite like this recruit and hoped he never would again. He was a challenge, but one he could handle. Maybe he should tell the staff weenies… but not yet. DID I JUST SAY THAT RECRUIT HAD YELLOW EYES? the Senior—with a sharp intake of breath—remarked to himself.

Experience had shown the drill instructors that in the summer months they received recruits from the school halls—and in winter months, from the pool halls. He wasn't sure behind which locker, or under which pool table they had found Recruit Parker, but it had to be one of a kind!

Chapter 19

GOD, ARE YOU LISTENING?

The next Sunday morning again delivered only one extra hour of sleep, but Pepper and the other recruits took whatever they could get. As their platoon marched to the chapel, Pepper checked the parking lots for any sign of the Catmobile or a friendly face from home, but all he saw was more recruits and drill instructors.

Inside, members of the platoon about to graduate sat in the chapel's place of honor and smiled knowingly at the other recruits. Together they listened as the chaplain explained, "I am your pastor and confidant while you are here at Parris Island. I am interested in your spiritual and personal growth. However, I am not a quick and easy way out of here. I will not let you give up on yourself, your family or your country. I will do everything in my power to help you become a Marine."

Pepper listened closely as one of the graduating recruits stood at the podium and read a poem called "Footprints in the Sand." The poem's comforting message is that when, in your hour of need, you only see one set of footprints, they aren't yours; they are the footprints of God carrying you. Following the reading, a group of recruits from the graduating platoon sang sweetly,

I know I've been changed

I know I've been changed

The angels in heaven have signed my name.

Pepper had visions of beautiful angels smiling and The Big Drill Instructor in the Sky watching over him as he faced the American flag and joined the congregation as they sang the Marines' Hymn from the Recruit Songbook. It was a sliver of comfort but just what the souls of the bedraggled recruits needed.

Later, after weighing all the things the chaplain had said, Pepper decided he was just another drill instructor in disguise. Like everyone else, the chaplain probably wouldn't believe his story about being an accidental recruit, and then he would be in double trouble with his new drill instructors.

Pepper's only hope was that Jessie Lee, Bubba Billy or one of his pals would come to his rescue. They were probably busy now, making plans for Thanksgiving. Jessie Lee would cook the biggest bird on the block. The table would be loaded down with all their favorite food, but his place would be empty. He was all alone. They will have forgotten him.

That night Pepper dreamed of being found and smothered with kisses by Fluffy and Jessie Lee, who whisked him home to his bed that had been calling to him: Pep-per … Pep-per. A full apology would arrive from the Commandant of the Marine Corps, and all would be right in his world. Dream on little tomcat.

The next day started just like all the others—total chaos! Although Pepper had visited the base many times and was familiar with the territory, he couldn't make a move without the drill instructors noticing. Also, he knew if he tried to escape and failed, there would a healthy dose of DISCIPLINE waiting for him in one of his most un-favorite places called the Pit, a large outside sandbox. Every minute of every hour of every day was filled with things to do, done so fast they went by in a blur. Catnaps were only a beautiful memory, and his eight-hour snoozes in the sun were replaced with all work and no play.

"What's happened to the happy-go-lucky cat I used to be?" Pepper asked himself. "Where are the fun and games? Warrior training is not fun! This is work, and I want to go home. At least there all my needs are met, and my mistress prepares meals just the way I like them and when I like them! I want my own special place in the sunshine where love, treats and catnip are in good supply, plus a big bowl of Jessie Lee's chicken 'n dumplings with my name on it."

Chapter 20

WHAT WE HAVE HERE IS A FAILURE TO COMMUNICATE!

"Just so we know who's the boss, Mister Drill Instructor," Pepper began, "this recruit has made a list of things that are non-negotiable. However, until Jessie Lee shows up, he will try to fit some of the other stuff into his busy schedule."

Pepper unfolded the list he'd prepared the night before and handed it to Sergeant Skittles, the Second Hat. The scratching on the note was barely legible but the man in charge played along. The note read:

TO WHOM IT MAY CONCERN:

ONE, I'm naturally a night cat, and I don't like to be awakened from my nap too early in the morning unless you can offer something interesting, such as food, catnip or a moving target. Otherwise, I can be rather testy.

TWO, I like it nice and quiet when I'm taking my naps and a high perch is my preference, so dibs on the top rack.

THREE, I prefer not to shower because I'm a self-cleaning machine. However, personal grooming is high on my list of things to do, and I'll need extra time for my nails.

FOUR, I prefer a nice mix of the high-priced Iams or Science Diet cat food topped off with a tasty slice of chicken. Hard cat food should be in good supply and available to me at all times.

FIVE, the Commandant of the Marine Corps says "recruits WILL be treated with firmness, fairness, dignity and compassion," so I'll be expecting a lot of respect from everyone in charge!

"Yessir", Pepper added, "I think I might like it here at Parris Island. The food is fascinating, and the woods and marshes have endless possibilities! And I would look dynamite in a set of dress blues! Look out ladies, here I come!"

The exasperated Hat nearly choked when he read the list. His first instinct was to pick the recruit up and throw him so far he would be in orbit. But true to his oath—and a large dose of common sense, he prevailed.

RECRUIT PARKER, Sergeant Skittles began, YOUR STUPID LIST OF FIVE NASTIES SMELLS SO BAD I WANT YOU TO PUT IT IN YOUR SKIVVIES AND KEEP IT THERE WHILE YOU DROP AND

GIVE ME FIVE PUSH-UPS FOR EVERY POINT. THAT WILL BE TWENTY-FIVE! DO YOU HAVE A PROBLEM WITH THAT, RECRUIT?

"Sir, this recruit will try, but he isn't sure the list will stay in his skivvies. You see, this recruit's skivvies are too large, and it's all this recruit can do to keep them up as it is."

NO EXCUSES RECRUIT, shouted the Hat. DROP AND GIVE ME TWENTY-FIVE PUSH-UPS OR THE ENTIRE PLATOON WILL JOIN YOU! IS THAT WHAT YOU WANT?

With every recruit staring at Pepper, he had no trouble reading their minds. *GET IT DONE OR YOU'LL HAVE TO DEAL WITH US*. Pepper dropped to the floor and started pumping his scrawny little arms.

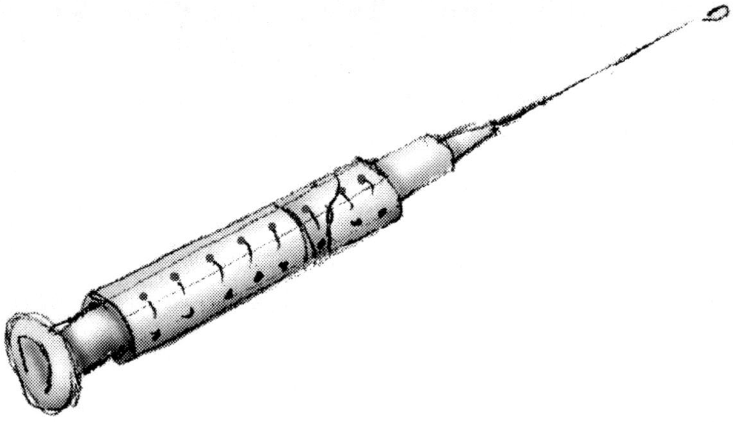

Chapter 21

INSPECTION OF BODY PARTS

"No, thanks, Doc," the accidental recruit stated emphatically. "This recruit doesn't do well with thermometers in his mouth or anywhere else! This recruit needs to be free of obstacles in case a catfight breaks out."

In spite of Pepper's protests, the doctor poked and prodded every inch of his body. He made a note concerning what appeared to be a closed seam on the side of the patient's stomach—probably an old scar. It was also noteworthy that the patient was covered with an abundance of black or white hair. Not a health issue, but it probably created havoc in his personal life. Other than exceptionally small feet and a spine that was unusually flexible, the doctor found the recruit to be in good condition.

"This will be your first in a series of shots," droned the doctor. "It won't hurt, but you will feel a little pinch."

"This recruit told you!" warned Pepper. "He does not need any shots because his veterinarian just gave him his rabies, feline leukemia and distemper boosters. And besides, Jessie Lee always manages to rub in Revolt-A-Bug once a month to take care of the flea and tick situation. So, let's be reasonable, and we can avoid a catfight! Meow!

"Well, Doc, that wasn't so bad," Pepper said after he stopped yowling. "Now that the small 'pinch' is over, would you care to share a dab or two of SOS with me for those aggravating no-see-ems?"

RECRUIT PARKER, called Sergeant Skittles, who was now standing in the doorway. DON'T MAKE ME HAVE TO COME AFTER YOU!

Ignoring the drill instructor, Pepper whispered to the doctor, "Where are my treats? I always get treats when I go to the vet!"

I'M THE ONE HANDING OUT TREATS, AND YOU'LL FIND THEM IN THE PIT, smiled the Hat.

"And how many push-ups would you like, Sir? You want them done in the Pit? You don't mean that big sandbox behind the barracks? The one this recruit has been using as a REAL sandbox? Oh, yuck," sighed Pepper as he headed for the door.

Chapter 22

PET PALS TO THE RESCUE

Meanwhile, back at the Happy Hideaway, the Pet Pals reviewed their plans to rescue P-2 while devouring another heavenly feast, compliments of Big Bill and Marvin.

The little clubhouse was now crowded with Pepper's friends and neighboring alpha cats and dogs. Many of the animals drifted in and out, hoping to keep up on what was going on while they enjoyed a free handout.

Fluffy, the white drama queen feline, joined Wendy, the tabby, as she meowed her own version of a Celtic song. Ricky Raccoon and Winston, the Yorkshire terrier, offered their suggestions on who should do what and in what sequence to rescue their leader. Jesse, the Border collie, offered to herd the drill instructors away from the recruits while Bubba took Pepper away.

Patrick, the Doberman pinscher in charge of logistics, searched the AMVETS and the Happy Hideaway clubhouse for the biggest backpack he could find. After that mission was accomplished, he kept searching the surrounding area and found a small JetSki someone had left behind the Post. Patrick would have preferred an aircraft of some sort but settled for the JetSki. After a thorough inspection, he made the necessary repairs to insure it was sea-worthy enough for Bubba to use in his rescue attempt. Several of the larger Pet Pals, Jesse and Ramey, helped him drag it down to the Sands beach at Port Royal.

Hours later, the Pet Pals had decided on a plan.

First, Bubba would use the JetSki to get to the shore of the Parris Island prison where Pepper was incarcerated. Second, once he located his brother, Bubba would use a claw to pick the locks that were holding Pepper hostage. And third, he'd provide a large treat to distract the drill instructor and a small one for P-2 to give him a little nourishment until Bubba could get him out of harm's way.

Naturally, once Jessie Lee saw her darling boy Pepper, she would have a field day cooking up lots of crabs, oysters, shrimp and a nice big bowl of chicken 'n dumplings just to bulk him up after he showed up starving and looking all pitiful-like.

Continuing his packing, Bubba added a nice big bag of treats and a flask of SOS in case the no-see-ums were on the prowl. The vicious pests didn't always bite because they were hungry, but because they loved their tasty victims' reactions. Humans would dance around, slapping and scratching until their skin bled, while animals would roll over and over on the ground trying to get rid of them. Many Marines at the AMVETS had sworn the no-see-ums were one of the Marine Corps' secret weapons—a biting torture that had broken the spirits of many recruits. In fact, several retired Marines at the AMVETS had told the Happy Hideaway members stories about how a large swarm of no-see-ums had actually carried a recruit into the woods and fed off him for days. Some nights they even heard his cries long after taps had sounded across the waterway.

By early morning the group had helped Bubba Billy pack the rest of the essentials needed for Pepper's rescue. With the plan worked out, Bubba puffed his chest out and saluted the Pet Pals. He would do them proud! While several of the club members gassed up the JetSki for the rescue, Fluffy and Francine made welcome home banners. Bubba curled up in a corner of the room to catch a quick catnap. "Life is good!" he purred.

Welcome Home P2!!

Chapter 23

BUBBA BILLY'S BIG ADVENTURE

While Bubba was resting, the Pet Pals had devised a perfect way for Bubba Billy to hide in plain sight of the Marines while keeping P-2 under surveillance. Last night Marvin had snitched a small scrap of camouflage material from the Depot Tailor Shop, and Francine, with a little snip here and a notch there, had made the perfect poncho. Bubba would all but disappear! An act of pure genius! The black cat would be incognito and blend in with all the other camouflage stuff the platoon had to drag around.

It was three o'clock and way too early in the morning for Bubba to be roused from his customary eight-hour nap. But he was about to embark on a secret mission to save his brother from the Marine Corps and bring him home safely. That took precedence over a leisurely nap; and, naturally, P-2 would have to pay the piper once he was signed, sealed and delivered into Jessie Lee's waiting arms.

When they returned, Bubba expected to be treated like a hero. Everyone would call him Mister Cat instead of Pepper. The territory and all the goodies would be his—at last!

The best part was that their mistress, Jessie Lee, didn't yet know that her sweet Pepper was gone, being held prisoner and possibly even starving to death. (Besides deleting his brother's phone message last Thursday morning, Bubba had hidden P-2's letters.)

After shoving his essentials into the backpack, Bubba strapped it onto the JetSki. Approaching the base by water was quicker than making the long trek through the main gate and the causeways. Besides, his backpack was too heavy to carry a long distance. The JetSki was a better choice. He could hide it in the bushes near the dock at Traditions, a Parris Island nightclub and restaurant. There it was isolated from the rest of the base where Pepper was probably being held captive. Bubba's back-up plan was that if something went wrong, he could always find a friendly handout at the club or a place to hide.

The Beaufort River was calm, but a heavy fog caressed the water, slowing the progress of the little craft as Bubba made his way from The Sands beach at Port Royal across the river to Parris Island.

Arriving at the Marine dock later than he had expected, Bubba dragged the JetSki onto the shore and into some nearby azalea bushes. It was time to be a hero! Bubba salivated as he took one of the treats out of his stash and popped it into his mouth. Yum! That tasted like another one... and another one.

Several hours later, Bubba awakened, yawned and stretched the full length of his body. It was time for action. But where could his brother be at this time of the morning?

"The mess hall," Bubba thought to himself, "that's the ticket! I'll go to the mess hall and wait for Pepper to show up. Sooner or later all the recruits and drill instructors have to eat."

Bubba wore his new camouflage cloak as he pussyfooted his way into the mess hall. He found the highest fixture and climbed to the top, a perch from which he could survey the area and pick out his brother from the crowd of look-alikes.

"There he is!" Bubba exclaimed to himself. "But wait just a minute! They're feeding him a Jessie Lee-type breakfast! Worse yet, he's inhaling it! There's something wrong with this picture! A feast of milk, eggs, ham, bacon, grits, potatoes, pancakes and syrup? This doesn't look like prison grub. Where's the bread and water stuff!"

As Pepper passed below Bubba's perch, the would-be rescuer could scarcely believe his eyes. "Good grief! What have they done to poor P-2's head! It's a high 'n tight, for heaven's sake! What else have they have done to the poor fellow?

"Pepper," Bubba continued to himself, "I take back all those wuss jokes I've made about you! You must be using that tail and whisker retraction trick Madam MoJoe taught us, because you're a lot taller than you used to be and—it's a fact—you don't even look like yourself! Which, personally, I think is a good thing.

"The good news is that the hair will grow back, and you'll be looking like your old self! But, little buddy, you might want to consider hiding in a closet for a few months after I get you home so you don't scare the ladies. Just looking out for you, little bro."

Bubba Billy followed the platoon back to the big brick building where the recruits were being held hostage. Still wearing his little camouflage poncho, he was able to sneak up the stairs and hide under a desk in the room where the warden and his men were talking.

They were laughing and joking about the incredible situations their accidental recruit had gotten himself into. One of their favorite stories was about the recruit disappearing into a tree and Sergeant Skittles' inability to climb up after him! His quick thinking had saved the day when he remembered how his own mother had threatened him with the fearsome word count, ONE, TWO, THREE! Before the number three became a word, the recruit had climbed out of the tree and hit the ground running!

Bubba's hair bristled when he realized they were talking about his brother. But there was nothing he could do at the moment. After that eye-opening observation, he realized that rescuing P-2 from the Marine Corps might be a little more difficult than he had first imagined.

YUMMY DONUTS

Chapter 24

GRITS AND GRIME

"The grits were extremely tasty this morning, Sir," Pepper purred to Drill Instructor Sergeant Clifton as the platoon left the mess hall. "If it's not too much trouble, this recruit requests a canteen of milk for the trip to the Thunder Dome at Leatherneck Field. And, if the drill instructor would fill up his pockets with treats for this recruit, he'll find that this recruit will perform much better. And the other recruits would like some donuts; that is, if it's not too much trouble."

SHUT YOUR MOUTH OR I'LL SHUT IT FOR YOU, shouted the Third Hat drill instructor. YOU ARE NOT ON A BOY SCOUT HIKE! DO YOU READ ME RECRUIT? DO YOU? ARE YOU TRYING TO FORCE ME TO BREAK THE U-C-M-J RULES AND GET COURT-MARTIALED? WELL, IT AIN'T GONNA HAPPEN ON MY WATCH! ASSUME THE POSITION! FIVE PUSH-UPS NOW AND FIVE CHIN-UPS WHEN WE GET BACK TO THE BARRACKS!

"Sir, this recruit's face is shut and his lips are sealed, Sir! What was that about a U-C-M-J or some cat named court-martial? Is that what we're having for lunch?" Pepper was puzzled, but in obedience to the Hat's command, he said out loud, "Yes Sir, the Pit would be just fine, Sir. And how many push-ups would you like this time, Sir? Before or after I make a deposit? Push-ups in the sand- box!" hissed Pepper to himself. "If she only knew, Jessie Lee would be amazed—and totally disgusted."

At that precise moment, a young lieutenant swung his new Jaguar XK8 convertible into a parking space several hundred feet away. Pepper continued doing his push-ups until the drill instructor yelled at him to come to attention and salute the officer.

DIDN'T YOU SEE THAT OFFICER, RECRUIT PARKER? WHY DIDN'T YOU SALUTE HIM? the Hat screamed at Pepper.

"Sir, Nossir, Mister Drill Instructor, Sir," responded the little recruit out loud. "The thought of saluting the officer hasn't been on this recruit's big list of things to do, and besides, he's too busy doing push-ups. But, of course, if it's something this recruit has to do to get closer to the main gate, you can count him in," Pepper muttered to himself. Aloud, Pepper called out, "Here little officer, these are for you. One salute, one push-up, two salutes, two push-ups.... And the list goes on." The Hat had to turn away so that the recruit wouldn't see him laugh. He had to give the little guy credit for trying to do two things at once.

Chapter 25

SPECIAL INTEREST

The saga of the unusual recruit, Pepper Parker, had not escaped notice. As though his strange appearance wasn't enough, the sometimes laughable situations he continually got himself and his drill instructors into went beyond the norm—even for a recruit. To make matters worse, the drill instructors might sometimes have embellished the stories into tall tales at the club. Recruit Parker was in a class by himself when it came to getting quarterdecked.

But Marine Corp recruit training was not a laughing matter. Before the odd recruit's training went too far, the drill instructors of Platoon 5001 decided it was time to apprise their Series Commander of the situation.

Going up the chain of command, Staff Sergeant Awesome also briefed Lieutenant Colonel Sharp, Commander of Fifth Battalion and Regimental Commander, Colonel Betelnut. The commanders and their staff listened closely as the drill instructor described the individual who claimed to be an accidental recruit in spite of the paperwork sent in by his recruiter, Staff Sergeant Gottaquota. The Platoon Log, Recruit Parker's Evaluation Card and the Recruit Incident Reports filed on him after each unusual occurrence or infraction of the rules were handed over. It was noted that the number of Page Eleven entries in Recruit Parker's Service Record Book had already set a record, and at the rate he was going, would set an all time high.

Colonel Betelnut kept a stern countenance as he listened to his staff's brief. He was concerned but considered many of the documented antics not only amusing, but possibly ingenious. Although he didn't want to lose a good recruit, if the situations his staff had described were true, it was a serious matter. Before briefing the General though, he would first make sure that Recruit Parker wasn't just a wayward recruit in need of more discipline. If not, he would then brief the General. An action passed was an action completed, but not before his drill instructors had put forth their very best efforts toward making the recruit into a Marine—or whatever else he might turn out to be.

The following day, Colonel Betelnut personally observed the strange recruit and found it prudent to apprise the Commanding General and his staff of his findings.

Apart from his peculiarities, they knew they had

a very special recruit on their hands. He couldn't be described in any general terms—he was just DIFFERENT.

He was really short, covered with black and white hair, had yellow eyes, and he didn't appear to move his lips when he talked. Also, his ears seemed to be a little closer to the top of his head than the sides.

He had no shoulders, which made it difficult for him to carry his rifle, but with the help of Velcro, he managed.

The good news was that although he was still claiming to be an "accidental" recruit, he tried hard to keep up with the other members of the platoon.

He was extremely intelligent and a fast learner.

He possessed a "can-do" attitude.

He was especially good at climbing and reconnaissance.

He was a natural-born fighter. A survivor.

His exceptional hearing and awareness had enabled him to alert his drill instructors to several dangerous situations involving venomous snakes and skunks.

He barely managed push-ups and pull-ups.

He didn't like taking showers like the other recruits

and had been observed licking himself clean after lights out by the fire watch. He even claimed his "tuxedo" was always the proper attire.

At the conclusion of the Colonel's brief, the General and his entire staff smiled. The possibility of having their very own secret weapon was electrifying. If that proved to be the case, it would require an exception to the Standard Operating Procedure.

The prospects were exciting, but considering Recruit Parker's peculiarities, it might be problematic for him to graduate as a "real" Marine. They would need to be creative. Perhaps acknowledge him secretly and encourage him to sign up for a career in Special Recon. The Commanding General asked to be kept up to date on Recruit Parker's progress.

While the staff weenies huddled in the head shed, Pepper continued to do his best. He was determined to finish what the indomitable Marine Corps Hats had started, because he wanted to make his mistress proud on graduation day. Just to see her one more time would truly be a gift from The Big Hat in the Sky—and maybe, just maybe, she'd take him home with her.

Chapter 26

PLAY NICE AND MIND YOUR MANNERS

Added to Recruit Parker's long list of transgressions was an extreme case of minding his manners. One day while marching back to the barracks from the mess hall, the platoon had to cross Boulevard de France, and Pepper was designated as one of the road guards. As the last member of the platoon cleared the road, Pepper turned to follow them, but not before taking notice of the gorgeous blonde in a red Miata sports car that had rolled to a stop. It had a blue sticker attached to the windshield on the driver's side, but Pepper only saw the beautiful lady. His smile was automatic, and being a southern gentleman, naturally he took his hat off. His chest puffed out, and he could feel himself growing taller and more handsome by the second. The lady smiled and waved. Recruit Parker returned her wave.

Expecting the road guards to rejoin their platoon across the road immediately, as ordered, the drill instructor was outraged that, yet again, Recruit Parker was not paying attention!

RECRUIT PARKER, DIDN'T YOU SEE THAT

SEDAN'S BLUE STICKER? ARE YOU TRYING TO EMBARRASS ME? WAS THAT THE GENERAL, RECRUIT? DID I SEE YOU WAVE?

"Sir, this recruit was just following General Order Number Ten: 'To salute all officers and all colors and standards not cased.' Sir, this recruit couldn't help himself. He didn't see a General, but he saw a lady, and she waved first! Jessie Lee taught this recruit good manners even before his eyes were open!

"'There's no excuse for bad manners' was her mantra, and she drummed it into this recruit and his brother from sunrise to sunset! Sir, this recruit was just being friendly! He didn't notice any sticker, but he is a gentleman—first, last and always!"

As the red sports car began to roll past them, the drill instructor came to attention and saluted smartly. Standard Operating Procedure had taught him that even if an officer was not in the vehicle, a salute was to be rendered to the blue sticker that signified the officer's ownership. But the rules didn't specify that he couldn't enjoy the view when the beauty behind the wheel waved and called out "Have a nice day!" as she drove off toward the commissary. The Hat took a deep breath, released the salute and turned back to the problem at hand—Recruit Parker. His shenanigans were especially frustrating, because they were always accompanied by a small element of truth or common sense.

The drill instructor marched the platoon back to their barracks where he would assign Recruit Parker a punishment to fit the crime.

NOW, RECRUIT PARKER, TO THE BULKHEAD! BECAUSE YOU DIDN'T SALUTE THAT BLUE STICKER, YOU WILL NOW SALUTE YOUR PLATOON, INDIVIDUALLY AND COLLECTIVELY! IF I SEE YOUR ARM DROOPING OR NOT SALUTING SMARTLY, THERE WILL BE FIFTY STRADDLE HOPS ADDED TO YOUR LIST OF THINGS TO DO! DO YOU READ ME? UNDERSTAND? DO IT NOW!

As soon as Pepper began to salute, the drill instructor glared at him and began another dressing down.

RECRUIT PARKER, asked the Hat, WHY ARE YOU SALUTING INDOORS? HUH? HUH? HAVEN'T YOU BEEN PAYING ATTENTION IN CLASS? YOU'VE BEEN INSTRUCTED NOT TO SALUTE INSIDE A BUILDING UNLESS YOU ARE UNDER BATTLE CONDITIONS! ARE YOU UNDER FIRE, RECRUIT? QUARTERDECK! FIVE CHIN-UPS! MOVE IT! NOW!

"Sir, this recruit is totally confused," grumbled Pepper. "Does the drill instructor want this recruit to salute or not? And while you figure it out, he'll just sit on his rack and catch up on the news."

As though a ghostly force had attacked, Pepper found himself at the bar, executing chin-ups until there was barely a chin left. After chow, Pepper was required to take his bucket outside and salute it until the drill instructor was sufficiently impressed to allow him back inside the barracks.

Sergeant Skittles didn't want to act like a crybaby by reporting the incident to the Senior Hat, but after a brewski at the club that evening, he couldn't wait to share it with his fellow drill instructors. This little scenario was a first. Good for at least a free drink for originality. His buddy, Sergeant Gleason, would fall off his chair laughing! Nevertheless, it was Sergeant Skittles' duty and joy to make Marines out of the bunch of Marine wannabes. Recruit Parker was a special challenge, but the Sergeant loved a challenge.

Poor Pepper was in a state of catatonic disbelief. He tried to make himself as small as possible to become one of the invisible recruits in the middle, but his story was too intriguing for the drill instructors to let slide. In fact, they were enjoying the challenge of making a Marine out of someone who claimed to be an accidental recruit. That was one for the books. An excuse they hadn't heard before.

With Madam MoJoe helping and the White Light surrounding him, Recruit Parker's spirit had begun to sing instead of whine. No matter how many hours their drill instructors kept the recruits on the drill field, he didn't complain. The big cat's boots didn't seem to touch the pavement, yet he was miraculously in step with the platoon. His rifle and gear didn't weigh him down like they had before. He felt taller and, to his surprise, seemed to be adapting to the Marine Corps way of life. But his inner voice told him he was still in the wrong place at the wrong time and that his new catitude would be temporary. He just needed to focus on whatever worked to keep the drill instructors off his back.

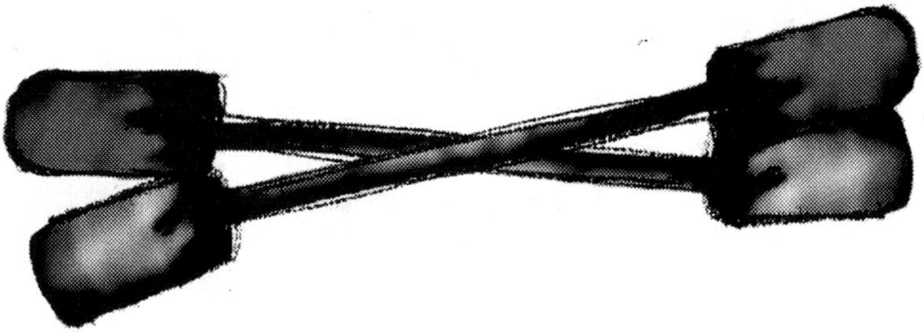

Chapter 27

FUN WITH PUGIL STICKS

The busy days became a blur as the three Hats kept their charges busy with relentless rounds of drill, chow, drill, run, chow, instruction, exercise, drill, drill, hike, chow and more drill. During something called free time, the recruits studied, cleaned their rifles and gear and wrote that important letter home.

No matter what they imagined might happen, it didn't—at least not when or where they expected it: like the pre-dawn, one-mile warm-up run yesterday that took them to an exercise field swarming with no-see-ems and instructors.

Under the moss-draped live oaks, the recruits had been armed with flak jackets, external padded jockstraps, padded horse collars and football-type helmets with mask guards. The weapon, called a pugil stick, was a long stick padded at each end, with the red end signifying a bayonet. The recruit's goal was to land two "killing" blows before his opponent did the same to him.

"It's not nice to fool Mother Nature, Sir," offered

Recruit Parker. “What’s this noise about hitting the other recruits with those silly looking sticks? This recruit has already explained to the drill instructor that he has eighteen self-sheathing bayonets. He doesn’t need any pugil stick! Besides, it wouldn’t be fair. The drill instructor needs to remember that most of the other recruits have never been in a real fight—except for the ones they play on video screens.

AND HOW WOULD YOU KNOW THAT? Sergeant Clifton asked.

“Sir, this recruit does not consider fighting to be entertainment. In the real world, this recruit would avoid a fight unless it was absolutely necessary—like defending his territory. But I guess this recruit’s gotta do what a recruit’s gotta do.

“Please pass him a pugil stick and he’ll wait for the enemy recruit. When he charges through the bushes and around the curve this recruit will be jumping, hitting and moving so fast he’ll be invisible! He’ll whack the enemy up one side of the head and down the other, using his pugil like a paddle to deliver the death blow. If this recruit doesn’t get the enemy on the Bridge, he’ll get him at the Octagon or in the Pit.

“But let’s get something straight, this Pit isn’t the same as the big sandy one outside the barracks, is it? No? Just checking."

An upbeat Pepper then shouted, "Rocking 'n' rolling! Life is good, like it should! Just like bowling. Set 'em up; knock 'em down!"

The drill instructors gathered around the fight area didn't know whether to laugh or cry when the strange recruit made the killing blow of the match. IT'S NEVER THE SIZE OF THE CAT IN THE FIGHT, they mused; IT'S THE SIZE OF THE FIGHT IN THE CAT! AND PARKER IS GROWING EVERY DAY!

Later on, back at the barracks, a mournful Pepper wrote:

Dear Jessie Lee,

This recruit keeps hoping there will be a letter for him at mail call, but so far his name hasn't been called. He's worried that something bad has happened to you. I hope you aren't sick, locked up or been in an accident. I prayed for you in chapel today.

This week we learned a lot about Marine Corps history, initial drill, values and pugil sticks. Next week we'll have our pictures taken, and I'll save one for you if you want one to remember me by.

I thought I saw Bubba Billy on an overhead pipe in the mess hall and later with Fluffy under a big oak tree. Tell him I'll see him when I see him, and I'll even give him a running start.

Love, Your little boy,

Pepper

Chapter 28

THE GAS CHAMBER

After spending the previous day clustered around the instructors, learning how to read maps, today's early morning hike was a welcome relief to Pepper and the rest of his platoon.

With the three Hats leading, the recruits chanted:

HERE WE GO. HERE WE GO,

ON THE MOVE,

IN THE GROOVE, IN THE GROOVE.

HERE WE GO, ALL THE WAY,

EVERY DAY!

As the recruits hiked down the road and through the trees, they had no idea where they were going or what was on today's menu. Soon, though, they got a hint when they passed a sign announcing the "Gas

Chamber." The main course would be instruction about the gas chamber and, for dessert, a large helping of nuclear, biological and chemical agents.

NO TRASH IN THE MASK, shouted the instructor. GET INTO YOUR OVERGARMENT, BOOTS, HEAD HARNESS, MASK, HOOD AND GLOVES! WHEN YOU COME OUT OF THE CHAMBER, DO NOT TOUCH YOUR SKIN ANYWHERE! DO YOU HEAR ME? DO YOU UNDERSTAND?

As the recruits helped each other with their gear, they didn't know that some of them wouldn't just walk out of the chamber. They would be begging to be released from their fiery, stinging hell. Many would even jump about and jabber unintelligibly while trying to get their masks off. Others would follow instructions and panic only after leaving the Gas Chamber.

With his heart racing, Pepper suited up and reluctantly followed the other recruits through the gray door bearing the Marine Corps emblem. The cinderblock chamber had several small windows, but Pepper noted they were up too high to enable him to climb out in full gear.

The door slammed shut, and the instructor ordered them to close their eyes and take a deep breath before putting their masks on. Then he released two canisters of gas. Immediately, the room became a rotten, foul-smelling stinging unbearable hell. Pepper and the other recruits had been instructed to hold their breath, take off their masks, put them back on and then take them off, again and again. In the process, a small amount of the gas had come in contact with the exposed skin of several recruits, and they panicked, screaming to be released into the fresh air. It was a little easier for Recruit Parker, because his fur absorbed most of the gas before it got to his skin. All the same, he was not looking forward to the nightly clean-up, because he would probably get violently sick if he swallowed any of the awful gas. Trying to think positively, Pepper conjured up visions of the nice warm shower he'd come to tolerate that would wash away most of the hateful rotten egg stench and burning sensation.

In another life, Pepper had marked his territory with his own scent and on occasion investigated some putrid odors other animals had left behind, but the horrible stench in the Gas Chamber was worse than that of ten skunks!

The special instructors stayed in the Gas Chamber with the recruits for the required three minutes, doing their best to calm those who were crying, screaming and frantically beating on the door to be let out. After what seemed an eternity, the door was opened, and the group of hysterical recruits rushed out into the fresh air. Some continued to jump around and shake their heads, leaving a trail of tears and streams of mucus and vomit in their wake.

Trying to make the best of a bad situation, several of the recruits screamed OOH-RAH MARINE CORPS—but not Pepper! Without acknowledging their spirited shout, the Hat instinctively screamed in return, YOU HAD BETTER SHUT YOUR MOUTHS AND OPEN YOUR EYES! NOW!

"Pee-u-u-e-e!" hissed Pepper as he heaved large amounts of gunk onto the ground. His face felt as though it was on fire, and his eyes stung so badly they couldn't stop watering. He was not a crybaby, but in this time and place he was one among the many. If he hadn't been in so much pain himself, he would have enjoyed watching the writhing dances and jigs performed by many of the other recruits in their attempts to rid themselves of the burning gas masks. The instructors watched as Recruit Parker slipped out of his mask and curled into a ball.

Even though he had made it out of the Gas Chamber in one piece, the huge cat wasn't sure he could swallow any more of the "treats" the Marine Corps had in store for him. "Remember to breathe. Inhale. Exhale. Just another challenge," he meowed.

From his perch in a tall pine tree, Bubba Billy watched for the door of the camouflaged building to open and his brother to reappear. From the sounds of crying, yelling and screaming going on inside, it sounded as though they might be having quite a party. Not one he wanted to attend—but interesting. The wary cat had already decided that the Gas Chamber was not a place in which to party or, for that matter, attempt a rescue. One cat in trouble was already one too many. Bubba Billy decided to just hide and wait for a better time to try to rescue his brother.

Chapter 29

BRIMMING WITH CONFIDENCE

Week Three turned out to be yet another week from hell. The recruits, as they marched to the Confidence Course to "build character," chanted:

I LOOK TO THE FRONT, AND WHO DO I SEE?

A MOTIVATED DRILL INSTRUCTOR LEADING ME.

I LOOK TO THE REAR, AND WHO DO I SEE?

A SENIOR DRILL INSTRUCTOR PUSHING ME!

I LOOK TO THE RIGHT, AND WHO DO I SEE? A BUNCH OF CIVILIANS TRYING TO BE LIKE ME!

When they arrived, Pepper approached Staff Sergeant Awesome, came to attention and requested permission to speak.

The Senior looked down and asked, WHAT'S ON YOUR MIND, RECRUIT?

"Sir, during Commander's Time, Sir, this recruit requests he be taught the words to the Marines' Hymn. Later, when he goes on the Slide For Life, it might come in handy, Sir!"

ARE YOU PLANNING TO FALL OFF THE ROPE, RECRUIT?

"Sir, Nosir! This recruit just likes to plan ahead. He didn't expect to be a recruit in the Marine Corps or he would have learned the words ahead of time, Sir!"

Staff Sergeant Awesome shook his head in disbelief. UNBELIEVABLE! THE RECRUIT WAS STILL CLAIMING TO BE AN ACCIDENTAL RECRUIT BUT WAS, AT THE SAME TIME, PREPARING FOR THE UPCOMING CONFIDENCE COURSE'S SLIDE FOR LIFE!

The Confidence Course consisted of eleven obstacles, each one more challenging than the last. First came Dirty Name. The second, Run, Jump and Swing, was followed by the Inclining Wall. Fourth came the Confidence Climb and then the Monkey

Bridge. Sixth came the Tough One, followed by the Reverse Climb.

Maneuvering over the sets of wooden obstacles and rope-climbing challenges wasn't so bad, but when the little accidental recruit was faced with obstacle eight, the Slide for Life, he took a ragged breath of fear. If he didn't time this just right, the jig would be up, and he would land in the water. Normally, he could deal with getting wet, but this dirty swamp-like hole was nasty, and he didn't want to spend the rest of the day wet, muddy and smelling to high heaven.

With a plan in mind, Pepper took a few moments to judge the distance and the obstacles. It wouldn't be easy, but he figured he could do it—with a lot of luck.

Taking quiet comfort in his climbing ability, Pepper slid off the 30-foot tower down a rope slanted at a 45-degree angle over the smelly pool of water. He clung to the rope with a death grip as he shinnied upside down over the water. Then, hanging onto the rope for dear life, he pulled his way over to the other side. Somewhere behind him, Pepper heard his buddy, Recruit Skippy, fall into the water and begin singing the Marines' Hymn.

After surviving what the big cat had considered

his biggest hurdle, he displayed an unbelievable degree of confidence when he and his fellow platoon members moved on to obstacles nine, the Hand Walk, ten, the Arm Stretcher and last, but not least, obstacle eleven, the Skyscraper. All three Hats encouraged the recruits and granted them a thumbs-up and a hard-earned "atta-boy" when they finished.

Trying to gain self-confidence on the Confidence Course proved frustrating for many of the fledgling recruits, but that was only the beginning of the busy week the Hats had in store for them.

Seated on his footlocker with ink stick in paw, Pepper wrote, dutifully, sadly and hopefully:

Dear Jessie Lee,

Like every other week, this one was filled with surprises. First we learned about maps and stuff, then we passed in and out of the Gas Chamber, learned to strike and choke our friends and enemies, run, climb and push our way through the Confidence Course, learn important stuff about Marine Corps history and, finally, how to lead each other.

We went to church on Sunday, and this recruit prayed so loud he embarrassed his drill instructor. Mama Cat, this recruit doesn't cry at night anymore, but that doesn't mean he doesn't miss you and wonder why you haven't come to get him.

It's the end of Training Week Three and you'll have a Marine in the family if you don't do something quick! The Marine Corps started this mess, and it looks like this recruit may have to finish it.

Love, Your tomcat, Pepper

Chapter 30

MORNING COLORS

Eight o'clock on a Friday morning found Platoon 5001 standing across the street from Barrow Hall, the Command Building. The platoon wouldn't officially attend the Colors Ceremony until after the Crucible, but the Hats wanted their recruits to see the impressive ceremony. The recruits were also anxious to show off how smartly they could salute when the flag was hoisted up the flagpole.

While they waited for eight o'clock, the lively medley of tunes played by the Marine Band brought tears to Pepper's eyes, reminding him of his civilian buddies and the good times they'd had at Land's End, in downtown Beaufort, at Frogmore International Airport and anywhere else they could hang out.

The accidental recruit sneaked a furtive glance at the civilians gathered around the steps of the Command Building. Pepper knew that Jessie Lee had worked at Barrow Hall before she retired from Civil Service and, occasionally attended the flag ceremony, so there was a possibility she might be here. He hadn't seen Bubba Billy or Fluffy in several weeks. No mystery there.

If he saw Jessie Lee, Pepper had decided he would just make a run for her. The Catmobile would surely be nearby, and if he timed it just right, the drill instructors wouldn't dare break ranks to chase him. He might even make such a clean get-away, they wouldn't miss him before chow.

At one minute to eight, General James and his staff came out of the Command Building and took their places on the steps facing the flagpole. All the Marines and recruits saluted smartly as the Marine Band played the National Anthem, and the flag was raised to the very top of the pole.

When the ceremony came to a close, a forlorn Pepper resigned himself to the fact that neither Jessie Lee, nor the Pet Pals had come to rescue him. As the platoon marched away, he muttered to himself, "There's always tomorrow."

Once again, a disappointed Pepper wrote:

Dear Jessie Lee,

This is your tomcat, Recruit Parker. This morning this recruit's platoon went to Morning Colors at Barrow Hall. He had hoped to see you there, but it wasn't his lucky day.

This recruit hopes all is well with you and Bubba. If the camellias are blooming, this recruit was wondering if you might consider picking a few and bringing them to him here at Parris Island. They would look real pretty on the Senior Drill Instructor's desk. Also, this recruit knows his drill instructor would love to meet you—you being so pretty and all.

This recruit would love to hear from you so, if you can't come, would you please write to him? He gets so lonely and wonders why you aren't looking for him. Don't you want him anymore?

This recruit will always love you.

Pepper

Chapter 31

COMBAT WATER SURVIVAL

PHASE TWO

Like every other day since his unfortunate incarceration, Pepper hit the deck with the rest of the platoon before daylight, toed the line and followed all the barked orders he had come to know by heart. MOVE IT! NOW! ANY TIME!

ARE YOU EYE-BALLING ME, RECRUIT PARKER? Sergeant Skittles asked. REPORT TO SERGEANT CLIFTON FOR QUARTERDECKING!

The recruits' diet of chow, drill, run, drill, chow, instruction, drill, exercise, drill, march, chow and more drill, chin-up, sit-up, hike, drill, and chow seemed never-ending, but when they crawled into their racks at night, they fervently hoped that tomorrow would be better. To survive, they had to have hope.

Still, the poor recruits never knew what was coming next. New challenges just kept raining down on their heads. The sharp recruits sucked it up; the others sometimes panicked. That was the case this morning when the recruits were introduced to Combat Water Survival.

Pepper zoned out and just tried his best to follow orders, no matter how difficult. If the other recruits could do it, so could he—or he would at least give it his best shot. He still expected to be rescued, but for now he just wanted to keep up and avoid the eternal quarterdecking.

This fine morning he enjoyed an inside grin, because he had a secret weapon when it came to swimming. A little something that would stun and amaze the drill instructors and swim staff. This recruit knew how to get the job done!

Pepper's very first swim lesson took place early one morning just before sunrise and involved a pillowcase being thrown over the side of the Broad River Bridge. Two innocent kittens, Pepper and Bubba Billy, were inside. It had been a frantic fight for survival, and Pepper and Bubba Billy had won, making their way onto the sandy beach. Later that morning, they were found by an oysterman and taken to the animal shelter from which Jessie Lee adopted them. Compared to that escape, anything else would be a piece of cake, and Pepper was already looking forward to the drill instructors' looks of astonishment. Their cries of AMAZING, RECRUIT PARKER! would burst from them like thunder.

After sitting through hours of instruction alongside the island's 60-meter indoor pool, Pepper stifled a yawn. When his turn came, he jumped into the pool with the other recruits, stayed underwater for five seconds, then surfaced with his little legs churning like he was pedaling a bicycle three sizes too small. Then he turned and swam back to the edge of the pool. With a cautious eye on the recruits, one of the instructors stayed close to the Red Dog Phone to report any emergencies. There were none.

The swim instructors were flabbergasted at the little recruit's gutsy performance. While some of his buddies were crying out for the orange rescue Gumbo Boat, Pepper was singing "Splishing and a-Splashing" and chanting "piece of cake! Honor, Courage, Commitment! Semper Fi, Marine Corps!"

On the way back to the barracks, Pepper joined the other recruits in telling the world he was "feeling good, like I should!"

HOW DID HE DO THAT? The mystified drill instructors asked each other. THAT RASCALLY RECRUIT IS JUST PLAYING WITH US! WHAT DO WE DO NOW? They weren't ready to give up on the little recruit. He had shown them that he had the heart required to be a Marine, and with that, everything else would be secondary.

Chapter 32

MESS & MAINTENANCE (GRASS) WEEK

"Sir, this recruit would be proud to serve duty in the mess hall, Sir!" Pepper shouted at the top of his lungs. "This recruit knows his way around a kitchen, and since he's already up at Oh-Dark-Thirty, Sir, he would be more than happy to serve. Pick this recruit! Pick this recruit! Pick this recruit!"

AFTER THAT LUCKY SWIM QUALIFICATION, YOU'VE EARNED IT, RECRUIT PARKER, agreed the Senior Hat. FOR TODAY, YOU WILL TAKE ORDERS FROM THE MESS SERGEANT.

"Sir, thank you, Sir," Pepper shouted as loud as he could. "This recruit will work hard to live up to Senior Drill Instructor Awesome's requirements with no excuses. It will be an honor to serve all the delicious food prepared by the food service personnel, and he'll do it with style!"

SEE THAT YOU DO, the smirking Hat replied.

Pepper thought he'd died and gone to heaven. After months of marching, drilling, swimming, studying and setting a new record in quarterdecking, his mind was filled with all the delicious possibilities awaiting him at the mess hall.

"Just think," Pepper mused, "this recruit will be surrounded by endless jugs of milk, piles of hamburgers, boatloads of seafood, here a chick, there a chick, everywhere a chick-chick! Warm ovens to toast my paws and no drill instructors staring me down! Oh yes, life is so-o-o good!"

When the Mess Sergeant handed Pepper a white mess hat at Oh-Three-Hundred the next morning, his expectations soared.

"What's this, Sir?" Pepper asked. "Teeny-weeny white party hats?" Well, okay, but this recruit just spent the last hour grooming himself and there's not a hair out of place. Still, the hat is a nice touch—so let the feast begin!"

"Recruit," the amused Mess Sergeant ordered, "take that mop and shine the deck until I can see my pretty face in it. After that, you will scrape and clean out the cooking vats and man the dishwasher. Consider yourself lucky, because we've advanced in the Marine Corps. Recruits only wash the pots and pans." Looking more closely at the recruit's hairy arms, the mess sergeant suggested that Recruit Parker might be used as a mop himself.

"Sir, Nossir, this recruit has never been used as a 'furry mop,' Sir!" Looking at the mess sergeant with quiet understanding, the little recruit asked, "And at which end of the mess hall will this recruit start, Sir?"

After hours of swabbing, scraping, polishing and peeling everything in sight, the recruits were allowed to fill their trays with anything they wanted to eat. Without the drill instructors in their faces all the time, the recruits laughed or jokingly complained about what they had gotten themselves into when they joined the Marine Corps. Pepper didn't mention the fact that he was an accidental recruit because nobody believed him. Not knowing what would come tomorrow, they were just enjoying today with all its possibilities.

Too soon for the recruits, Sergeant Clifton materialized at one of the tables. He sipped a glass of water while he eyeballed his charges. The tough Mess Sergeant had given his recruits high marks for keeping the place spotlessly clean, keeping the count on deck, preparing salads and insuring the silverware was in place. Admittedly, he had been apprehensive about the strange recruit being assigned to mess duty. He would have preferred to have him outside mowing the grass or cleaning up in an area where he could personally keep an eye on him. But his gut feeling was wrong because Recruit Parker had fit right in and seemed to be totally committed toward getting the job done.

Chapter 33

MAGGIE'S DRAWERS

Peals of thunder and the crack of lightening strikes startled the sleeping recruits. Pepper sat bolt upright, leapt off his top rack and toed the line. He was not alone. Recruit Skippy and several other recruits were there as well. The next flash of lightening sent them scrambling back to their racks as the drill instructors looked on, in amusement, from the mirrored window in their house.

I'VE NEVER SEEN A RECRUIT MOVE AS FAST AS RECRUIT PARKER, affirmed Sergeant Skittles. I THINK HE'S IN LOVE WITH THAT WHITE LINE.

The thunderstorm that had moved over the barracks earlier in the morning had swiftly scattered out to sea, but another band of heavy rain had taken its place.

Too soon for the sleepy recruits, the Second Hat was screaming, IF IT AIN'T RAINING, WE AIN'T TRAINING! For added emphasis, he banged on his personal set of trashcans, whose lids flew off and hit the walls. One rolled down the drill instructors' highway, just like he'd intended.

TOE THE LINE AND GET YOURSELVES READY FOR A NICE LONG HIKE, he ordered.

By the time Platoon 5001 had eaten chow, enjoyed two hours of physical training and taken care of chores at the barracks, they were ready for a siesta. Naturally, the Hats had other plans, like a ten-mile hike to the rifle range situated on the other side of the Island.

MOTIVATION! DEDICATION!

TO THE CORPS! LEFT FOOT! YOUR GOOD FOOT!

THUNDER, LIGHTNING, DRIZZLING RAIN,

NOTHING BUT P.T ON MY BRAIN.

The weather at the rifle range was by now crisp and clear, perfect for firing rifles. But instead of getting right down to the shooting, what the recruits got were lots of boring lectures on Weapons Handling, Introduction to Marine Marksmanship and Fundamentals of Marksmanship. Pepper and the other recruits sat on six rows of backless wooden benches while an instructor used a blackboard to teach. After what seemed like an eternity, they actually got to shoot five rounds into a target to see if they had been paying attention in the class for BRASS-F, which stood for Breathe, Relax, Aim, Stop, Squeeze and Follow Through. Sergeant Clifton had even brought along an extra supply of Mister Velcro for Recruit Parker's rifle.

Pepper was feeling no pain as he kicked himself into high gear for the task at hand. He had been cleaning, polishing and carrying Rip, the rifle, with him everywhere he went for six long weeks. It was now time for old Rip to return the favor by blasting holes straight through the center of the target. Grudgingly, however, Recruit Parker soon realized that old Rip needed lots more training.

On the day of Final Qualification each recruit was issued live ammunition. Regulations prohibited them from playing with their bullets, but the recruits kept them in their hats and counted them repeatedly as though one of the bullets was going to jump into another recruit's hat and hang out. There were no stray full-metal jackets at Parris Island. Weapons Training Battalion personnel kept strict records of where each round of ammunition was issued, to whom, who fired it and where the casings were left.

Assuming the kneeling position, Pepper bragged to himself, “This recruit is locked ‘n’ cocked, rockin’ and rollin!” He’s got his rifle barrel smoked, earplugs stuffed way in and his sights on a teeny black blob. One shot, one kill, shoot the black, feel the thrill! Let ‘er rip, Rip!

“This recruit is looking for a ‘possible,’ and if Maggie’s Drawers pops up one more time, this recruit is gonna bust up that wicked red disk and hide it someplace the sun don’t shine,” muttered Pepper to no one in particular.

DO YOU HAVE A PROBLEM RECRUIT? asked the Line Coach. Checking Pepper’s rifle, he told him, BE SURE TO CHECK THE RANGE FLAG FOR THE CORRECT WIND DIRECTION AND THEN RESIGHT YOUR RIFLE. TRY IT AGAIN.

“Sir, thank you, Sir,” Pepper replied. “This recruit will take care of that riki-tik.

“Hey, Recruit Skippy,” called Pepper. “That was a nice shot!”

“Sir,” Pepper called out to his Senior Drill Instructor, “these recruits are good to go! Those bag nasties we had for lunch really hit the spot, and this recruit is one fired-up feline, Sir!”

I’D BE FEELING A LOT BETTER IF YOU WERE LESS FIRED UP AND MORE CAREFUL WHEN

YOU SQUEEZE THAT TRIGGER, RECRUIT, warned the Hat. SEE THAT YOU DO EVERYTHING BY THE BOOK. LIFE IS GOOD. DON'T SCREW IT UP!

Two huge red pennants fluttered from the flagpoles at either end of the line of targets, indicating to the world that the range was HOT—that live ammunition was being fired. The pennants also told the recruits which way the wind was blowing near the targets.

PLATOON 5001, LISTEN UP, Staff Sergeant Awesome shouted. THIS IS THE DAY THAT SEPARATES THE MEN FROM THE BOYS! ARE THERE ANY BOYS HERE?

SIR, NOSIR! shouted the platoon.

"Sir, Recruit Parker affirms that the drill instructors of Platoon 5001, Marine Corps Recruit Depot, Parris Island are totally awesome, Sir! Filled with inspiration, dedication and Corps to the bone! This recruit wants to grow up to be just like them, Sir!"

DREAM ON, RECRUIT! IT APPEARS YOU'VE HAD A GROWTH SURGE, BUT YOU'D BETTER KEEP YOUR EYE ON THAT TARGET OR BE ON A FIRST-NAME BASIS WITH THE BIG DRILL INSTRUCTOR IN THE SKY! DO YOU READ ME?

"Sir, in this recruit's dreams, Sir? A catnap would be nice! Yes Sir, Firmness, Fairness, Dignity and

Compassion for all!

"Good to go, Sir! This recruit just loves the rifle range after a tropical storm has blown through. It builds men with character! Yes Sir! If it ain't raining, we ain't training!"

ALL READY ON THE RIGHT? ALL READY ON THE LEFT? ALL READY ON THE FIRING LINE! SHOOTERS, COMMENCE FIRING! commanded the Range Officer.

After noting several missed attempts, the rifle instructor did a double-take when Recruit Parker fired a low but qualifying score. His drill instructors grinned and passed the hat to collect their bets. Madam MoJoe just smiled.

During the Final Qualification festivities at the rifle range, Bubba Billy and a large group of assorted Pet Pals had been sitting in or near a large oak tree overlooking the range. In varying degrees, they were truly amazed that Pepper was still there and even acting like a real recruit. News of his incarceration had spread like wildfire through the barrier islands and sleepy little towns of Yemessee, Beaufort, Port Royal, Frogmore and the other barrier islands.

At first the animals had just wanted to see what the big fuss was about, but after seeing Pepper in action, they had followed his platoon everywhere, watching and waiting. The females were continually swooning, and the males were giving each other high fives—all except Bubba Billy. He had failed to rescue his brother, but the band of Pet Pals hadn't given him any grief or even acted as though they cared.

Because Bubba Billy wasn't the center of attention, he snarled to the other spectators, "I've given P-2 plenty of opportunities for escape, and he's ignored them all. He acted like I wasn't even there!! Mind you, if there's any ignoring going on, it's gonna come from ME!" growled the big cat. "While P-2's playing at being a Marine, I'M the alpha cat, and I'm declaring it's party time! Let the good times roll! But before we leave, I'll just mail this letter to P-2 with lots of hearts and flowers drawn on the envelope for his drill instructor. Not that I want to get him into any trouble, but just to show him how much I care," grinned Pepper's brother with glee.

The days had turned into weeks and Pepper was still missing. Jessie Lee had posted pictures of him on the Internet and around town, asking for any information that would help her find him. She regularly checked the animal shelters and veterinary clinics to see if he had shown up, but no one had seen him. There was not much else she could do, but giving up on that sweet cat was not an option.

Maybe Big Bill over at the AMVETS has seen him. With that fragile hope, she drove to the Port Royal Post.

The laid-back, retired Marine was always glad to see Miss Jessie Lee, and it troubled him that she was so unhappy about her missing cat. He had even gone to the animal shelter and collected several kittens to take to her to replace Pepper, but she wasn't interested. Pepper couldn't be replaced any more than Bill's old bloodhound, Marvin, could be.

Meanwhile, back at the barracks, a dejected Pepper wrote:

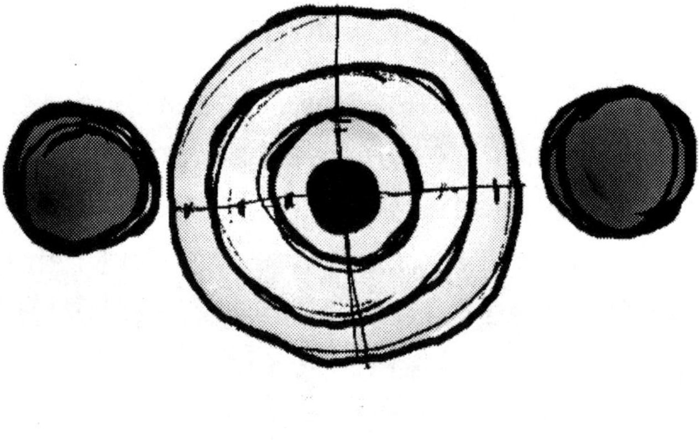

Dear Jessie Lee,

We went to the rifle range this week, and after a couple of wrestling matches with Maggie's Drawers (missing the entire target), this recruit finally qualified and didn't let his platoon or drill instructors down.

I'm so busy, but when mail call comes every evening and there's nothing there from you, I feel so bad I think about going AWOL. But the drill instructors warned me that they would find and court- martial me before I even made it home.

Jessie Lee, I know you love me and your letters just got lost in the mail. One little thing, Mama Cat, I would really appreciate it if you would tell Bubba Billy not to send me any more letters with kissy hearts and flowers for my drill instructors. They always thank him by giving me more push-ups in the Pit. I'm so tired my tail would be dragging if I didn't have to keep it hidden.

Love, your letterless cat, Pepper

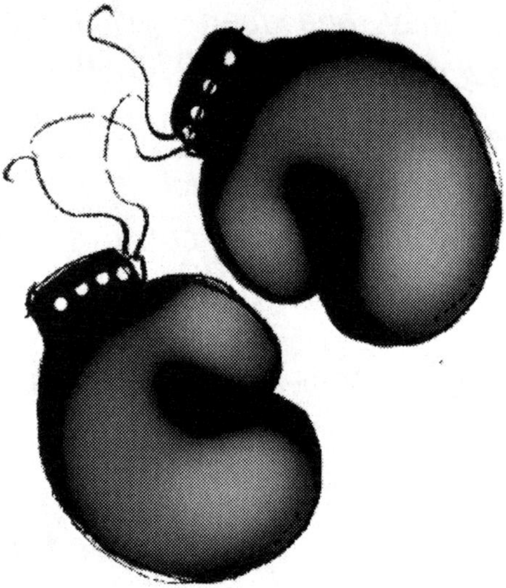

Chapter 34

COMBAT HITTING SKILLS

The recruits knew that they were in for yet another unforgettable day when Sergeant Skittles, the second Hat, gave them one of his special grins. GET OUTSIDE! he barked.

Soon the platoon was marching to the Thunder Dome and all the excitement it had to offer, chanting:

HERE AT PARRIS ISLAND,

RUNNING 'TIL I'M WET.

NO ONE'S EVER DROWNED IN SWEAT!

RUNNING FASTER, RUNNING LONG.

GETTING TOUGHER, GETTING STRONG!

MARINE CORPS. . . P.T.! RUNNING! OOH-RAH!

When they arrived, each recruit put on a three-sided, padded helmet, a padded external crotch protector and gloves. Then they faced another recruit in a three-sided, padded wooden ring not much larger than a coat closet. The Close Combat Instructor, wearing a black sweatshirt, began each fight.

ON MY WHISTLE, he directed each of the two recruits in the ring, YOU WILL EXPLODE! FIRST STRAIGHT PUNCH TO THE HEAD WINS. NO ROUNDHOUSES, NO UPPERCUTS, NO PUNCH TO THE TOP OF THE HEAD AND NO HUGGING. DO YOU UNDERSTAND?

“Sir,” Pepper informed the instructor, “This recruit doesn’t need to practice what he does naturally and this recruit does not consider fighting a game. Why, over in Beaufort, when this recruit walks down the street, the other cats and dogs respectfully get out of his way and call him Mister Cat! So what’s with those gloves, masks and plastic teeth? Don’t you know attack cats need no protection? They just go in, get the job done, then take a nap or enjoy a treat.

“And you expect this recruit to stand up on his hind legs and fight?” argued Pepper. “In case you hadn’t noticed, Sir, this recruit can fly through the air and land on his feet every time! One swipe of these razor-sharp claws will leave a wake-up message that will scar anyone for life, and you want this recruit to climb into that teeny-weeny space and fight? It just wouldn't be fair to the other recruit, Sir! I'd wipe him out! Cats don't stop fighting until the other cat is down! Even then, the top cat may give the loser one more swipe just for good measure."

DON'T TALK THE TALK IF YOU CAN'T WALK THE WALK, RECRUIT, responded the instructor.

Contrary to his words, Recruit Pepper landed the required blows to knock down his challenger, then stopped when the instructor blew his whistle and placed his gloved paws on the railing of the Fighting Pit.

Pepper's drill instructors were constantly amazed at what the little recruit accomplished. No matter how much he detested whatever task he was required to perform, he seemed to just do it and get on to whatever was next. It was like he was biding his time. But for what? Although he still insisted that he was not a real recruit, he managed to get by. Not anything to brag about, but considering his size, he was certainly pulling more than his own weight. In fact, he seemed to light up when he faced a challenge.

"Lordy, Lordy," the big cat hissed under his breath, "when this boot camp is over, you and the other Hats need to come home with this recruit, and he'll show you how REAL cats fight! Hear me roar! This recruit is ALPHA!"

Later, facing the second Hat, the accidental recruit asked, "Sir, has this recruit told the Drill Instructor lately that he doesn't belong here and that tonight he has a date at Harold's Club over in Yemessee? This recruit needs a ninety-six hour pass, because when this recruit's sweetheart is ready to party, he needs to be there! Time and pussycats wait for no tomcat, if the Drill Instructor gets this recruit's drift, Sir."

ARE YOU TALKING TO ME, RECRUIT PARKER? the Second Hat asked. JUST SO YOU KNOW, HAROLD'S CLUB IS ONE OF MY FAVORITE PLACES, AND I'LL MAKE SURE YOUR DATE ISN'T LONELY! BUT FIRST, SINCE YOU FEEL LIKE DANCING, REPORT TO SERGEANT CLIFTON AND GIVE HIM TWENTY SIDE-STRADDLE HOPS AND THEN TEN PUSH-UPS!

"Sir, Yessir! Back to the Pit, Sir! This recruit has spent so much time in the Pit, he plans to claim squatter's rights or get a homestead exemption tax credit on it!"

Chapter 35

HE CAN FLY! HE'S SUPER RECRUIT!

As Platoon 5001 marched up to the base of the 47-foot high metal tower, their eyes bulged out, and their mouths felt dry as a bone. The tower looked at least a mile high, and there was an anemic looking thread of a rope, with lots of rings attached, hanging off the side. Like tiny specks, the special instructors stood on top of the tower in their gray sweatshirts.

"Not looking good," thought Pepper. "Climbing is one of my strong points; unfortunately, climbing down isn't. Considering the height, though, I might have to put some rocks in my pockets just to weigh me down. Otherwise, this recruit could be swinging in the breeze clear into next week."

Even after listening to the reassurances given to them by the instructors, the fear of heights suffered by the recruits squatting in the school circle was not relieved.

After training, the instructors smiled as they placed straps on the recruits' wrists. They explained,

WE CALL THIS A SISSIE STRAP, BUT WE KNOW THAT AT PARRIS ISLAND THERE ARE NO SISSIES, RIGHT?

The recruits shouted loudly, SIR, RIGHT, SIR!

To show the recruits how easy it was to rappel off the tower, Sergeant Skittles climbed to the top and displayed what was generally known as the Dead Bug Leap. From the top of the 47-foot tower, he dropped off backwards without holding onto the rope that was tied around his waist. Halfway down, he yanked on the rope and stopped, facing the sky, with his body, head and arms hanging down. Then he came to life, zipped to the ground and walked off for a quick drink of water. The recruits were thrilled! Instead of dreading the jump, several rushed to be first off the platform. "If he can leap off without holding onto the rope," they thought, "then we can do it, too." But because they had promised their mothers to be careful, they decided they would hold onto the rope anyway.

The recruits climbed the stairs and lined up. As each stepped off the edge of the tower, he let loose the required OOH-RAH as he followed the drill instructor's leap into space.

Recruit Skippy was first to leap, and all too soon it was Pepper's turn. Recruit Parker repeated the command: ONE DOWN, ONE WRAP, TWO DOWN, LOCK THE GATE, THE GATE IS LOCKED! With his left paw guiding, Pepper loosened his grip and stepped over the edge, meowing “OOH-RAH! MARINE CORPS!” Landing on his feet, the cat recruit felt a rush of pure power. “Piece of cake! No mountain climbing* for me today!”

**Mountain Climbing: Running in place while in the push-up position.*

Classes on Camouflage, Cover and Concealment filled the hours before sunset and into the night. A bonus course on Field Sanitation was fitted into the recruits’ schedule while they camped out in the woods near the abandoned World War II airstrip at Page Field.

Instead of the bag nasties from the mess hall, the recruits enjoyed packages of Meals Ready to Eat, swapping for their favorites. “This food’s certainly not up to Jessie Lee’s standards,” Pepper grumbled, “but I guess it’ll have to do until I get home.”

Still hopeful, Pepper again wrote:

Dear Jessie Lee,

This week was a lot of fun. We rappelled up and down Holberton Tower, and this recruit enjoyed it. Then we went to Page Field where we camped out and gained knowledge about sanitation and stuff like that. I'm truly a tidy cat compared to some of the other recruits.

Mama Cat, this recruit still goes to chapel every Sunday, and he loves and thinks about you even if he still hasn't heard from you. Bubba and his buds hang around all the time now, but this recruit doesn't let them know they've been spotted. Time marches on, and we'll get everything straightened out when this recruit gets home. Please, please write to me.

Love, your adopted son,

Pepper.

Chapter 36

MISTER GRENADE IS NOT YOUR FRIEND!

On sets of bleachers under a stand of tall pine trees, Platoon 5001 assembled for a grenade lesson and demonstration. As expected, the recruits were shocked and awed by the incendiary grenade display. A few actually looked forward to their time in the Throwing Pits, but not Recruit Parker. Experience had taught him that nothing good would come from a loud noise or flash of light. The instructor confirmed his fear when he told them, THE DIFFERENCE BETWEEN TRAINING AND A LIVE GRENADE IS THAT ONE OF THEM WILL KILL YOU! DO NOT TRY TO FIX A GRENADE THAT DOES NOT GO OFF! UNDERSTOOD?

SIR, YESSIR! shouted the recruits in unison.

Pepper could barely conceal his fright at the Explosions and Bright Flares demonstration. The noises and things that previously would have sent him into fight or flight mode had almost become the norm, but he paid close attention to what the trainer was saying so that he could survive. Despite his outward bravado, Pepper was far from wanting to strap on his helmet and flak jacket and sit in the shed at the Hand Grenade Range. Hadn't that sign said DANGER! IMPACT AREA, KEEP OUT?

He wasn't alone. Pepper was just one of forty-four recruits crouched in a red cinderblock shed. Each one nervously awaited his turn in the Throwing Pit where they were expected to throw a live M-67 fragmentation grenade at a foxhole containing two enemy dummies—dummies that looked as though they had given up the ghost years ago.

When Pepper's turn came, the instructor reminded him to: ONE, TAKE THE GRENADE; TWO, PLACE YOUR THROWING HAND ON YOUR CHEST; and THREE, HEAD AND EYEBALLS STRAIGHT DOWN.

When the instructor paused and asked the recruit, WHAT TYPE OF GRIP? Recruit Parker shouted, "Death grip, Sir!"

OKAY, the instructor continued. ROTATE DOWN! FLIP YOUR HAND UP AT A 45-DEGREE ANGLE AND THROW!

REMEMBER, THERE ARE NO SLEEPING BEAUTIES! ALL GRENADES ARE LIVE!

Pepper followed the instructor's directions, pulled

the pin and quickly threw the grenade as far as he possibly could. It almost stopped short before rolling into the foxhole. Pepper had scored a hole in one! From the shed, he could hear his platoon cheering, and he caught the three happy Hats trying to cover up a smile nasty!

Later, a brave Pepper wrote again to his beloved mistress:

Dear Jessie Lee,

This is probably the last letter I'll write to you because I'll be leaving for the Crucible tomorrow morning. It's going to be a real nightmare in the woods, but I don't want you to worry. The drill instructors have trained me and the rest of my platoon to be the best we can be, and I know we'll make them proud. Just keep your fingers crossed for me.

It won't be long now before I'll graduate and be able to walk off Parris Island without someone calling me a quitter. I'll stop by the house to see you before I go on my way. Mama Cat, you know I'd never want to be a bother to you. Just sleep well at night knowing that soon I'll be helping to defend our country.

All my love,

Pepper

Chapter 37

TROUBLE IN BUBBA-LAND

Three significant things happened on Wednesday, the fourth of December. First, Platoon 5001 left their home at Fifth Battalion for the Crucible exercise. Second, there was a little incident at Parris Island that caught local and national media attention. And third, Bubba Billy got busted!

It all happened the day the mailman changed his schedule and made an early deposit in the mailbox in front of the little brick house where Jessie Lee and her cats lived.

Since Pepper's unfortunate incarceration at Parris Island, Bubba Billy had dutifully lain in wait for the mailman, checking for any letters from Pepper. Being a considerate brother, he had then squirreled them away because he didn't want their mistress to get all upset. The fact that his endeavor was totally self-serving didn't bother him but, if it did, he dismissed it without a care. He just needed a little more time to cement his role as the alpha cat of the neighborhood, and Pepper's return wasn't going to help him one bit.

CATMOBL
REDSKINS

It had been almost two months since Pepper's disappearance, and Jessie Lee had grown so depressed that she'd sort of let herself go. Her weight had dropped to just over a hundred pounds, and now her favorite gray sweatpants were at least two sizes too large. An equally loose-fitting, red Washington Redskins sweatshirt and well-worn tennis shoes completed her ensemble. She had climbed into these feel-good clothes this morning to face yet another day without her precious cat.

With the radio tuned to her favorite beach, boogie and blues station, her feet shuffled to the beat of the shag music while she swept the floor. An hour later, she was outside working in the yard when she saw the mailman. Hurrying out to collect the early mail delivery, she murmured her daily prayer that this was the day someone had found her precious Pepper.

Bubba was on the screened-in porch, snoozing in a perfect pool of warm sunshine. He had heard his mistress go outside but thought nothing of it. His ears flicked slightly, however, when he heard her return. He couldn't tell if she was laughing or crying when she ran into the kitchen and grabbed the car keys. Following the slam of the back door, the next sound Bubba heard was the Catmobile being fired up. His mistress was probably going to Hardee's for a ham biscuit and grits.

Jessie Lee backed the Catmobile out of the carport so fast that the right fender ripped off a large chunk of a post holding up the roof. The screech of tires and smell of burning rubber that followed left no doubt that the driver was in one heck of a hurry. "She must really be hungry," the big cat concluded.

Bubba took his time as he stretched, yawned and then moved stealthily to the kitchen door to see what had caused the ruckus. He was too late! There on the kitchen floor was an opened letter from Pepper! Bubba's fear factor went into overdrive; he knew his fragile house of cards had just crashed and burned!

Pulling himself together, Bubba set about picking up the pieces of his plan to be Pepper's replacement as the neighborhood alpha cat. He figured Jessie Lee could take care of herself, and he had to get to the clubhouse as soon as possible. He had a long way to go and a short time to get there if he was going to do damage control before the situation got totally out of control.

Bubba Billy skidded to a stop outside the club and took a moment to catch his breath and collect his thoughts. A peek in the window revealed that Fluffy, Ramey, Ricky and Francine were making a huge welcome home banner for Pepper. Marvin, Jesse and Winston were comparing notes on each other's escapades of the night before. Tabby-cat Wendy practiced her improvised Celtic woman solo, while others tried to zone out and catch some z's in a warm place.

It appeared that the gang's plans for the day and possibly into the night included a picnic at Parris Island and some serious Pepper watching. Marvin had traded favors for a copy of the training schedule, and it revealed that this week Pepper's platoon would be in its last phase of training. Next on the recruits' agenda was something called the Crucible. The Pet Pals had already picked out several perfect spots along the route from which to watch. Their spies revealed that it would take Pepper two and a half days to get through the woods and all the obstacles the Marines had put up for him. Still, they kept the faith that their leader would easily make it. Granted, nothing was guaranteed, but they had high hopes that Alpha Cat Pepper would soon be on his way back to the hood. The welcome home banners were already hung in the clubhouse; band members of the "Meowing Sensations" and "The Detonators" were waiting for their call.

Bubba didn't bother to tell them about the terrible scene he had witnessed back at the house when Jessie Lee had taken off for Parris Island to rescue her darling cat. He needed to use the time he had left to flatter the ladies, arm wrestle the males and do whatever else it might take to boost his claim to alpha cat status.

Chapter 38

POSSIBLE TERRORIST ATTACK!

Jessie Lee wasn't in the mood to waste time chit-chatting with the Marine sentry when she arrived at the Parris Island Main Gate. Instead, she just put the pedal to the metal, sped through the gate and roared onto the causeway to find her sweet, darling cat. Pepper's letter was barely legible, but from the return address, she knew exactly where he was being held captive. Although his letter didn't sound as though he was being mistreated, the Marine Corps had no business capturing her cat and not telling her. She was going to fix that situation right now, and by the time the sun went down, she was determined to have him safely at home.

As the vintage white Cadillac Eldorado passed through the main gate without stopping, the sentry immediately activated General Order #3, which directed him "to report all violations of orders I am instructed to enforce."

The sentry sent a chase car to intercept the out-of-control vehicle. Then he called the Corporal of the Guard to report the incident. Historically, recruits might try to get off the base, but the sentry had never personally known of anyone crashing the gate to get in! Always on alert, the Marines never knew when the war in Iraq might show up at their door, but they were always prepared. The driver of the car appeared to be a civilian woman, and the glazed look the sentry had seen in her eyes spoke volumes. This woman was on a mission!

With sirens blaring and flashing blue lights visible in her rearview mirror, Jessie Lee sped towards the one place she was sure to find help—Barrow Hall. The General would certainly want to know about the little shenanigan his drill instructors had pulled and would put a stop to it immediately! He would have his Chief of Staff put the entire base on notice that Recruit Parker was not to be harmed but brought to his mistress immediately so that she could take him home where he belonged.

As the Catmobile approached Barrow Hall, Military Police cars had already blocked Jessie Lee's entry to the command building's parking area. With guns drawn, the MPs crouched beside their sedans and ordered the driver of the Cadillac to halt and step away from the vehicle. If they thought this driver was going to cooperate, they had another think coming, because the mile-long Eldorado merely did a wide U-turn around Iron Mike and headed for the Fifth

Battalion barracks, where her precious Pepper was being kept hostage.

Again, the Military Police gave chase with sirens screaming and blue lights blazing. Rows of startled seagulls took flight as Jessie Lee took a shortcut across the Peatross Parade Field. She drove the Catmobile up to the very steps of the barrack's doorway, jumped out and was inside the squad bay before those in pursuit could stop her. Naturally, when the Sergeant Major and Sergeant of the Guard saw a female senior citizen in total disarray at their office door, they rendered her every military courtesy.

"Good morning, Ma'am," they said in unison. "How

may we be of assistance?"

"You can get the tomcat you call Recruit Parker and bring him to me before I do something we'll all regret!" the hysterical woman shouted, desperately wringing her hands.

Shrugging, the Marines looked at each other, trying to make sense of what she was saying. If they were being accused of holding her tomcat hostage, then they had better produce said tomcat before she did something terrible.

"I'll give you to the count of three!" she warned. One!" The Marines were alert but uncertain about what to do to bring the situation under control. As it happened, they didn't have to do anything except step aside for the MPs who were racing with guns drawn down the hallway to take the terrorist down.

DOWN ON THE FLOOR! they shouted to Jessie Lee. NOW! ON THE FLOOR, AND DON'T YOU DARE MOVE!

Jessie Lee, knowing she was outnumbered, did as she was told, although it wasn't easy to keep her dignity in place when she was lying face down on the floor with at least six hundred military policemen hovering over her. While she was nose to nose with the floor, she noticed how clean it was and made a mental note to inquire about what cleanser the

Marines used.

Then, as if on cue, Jessie Lee leapt to her feet and screamed her way into a full-blown rage! That got everyone's attention, because it was not a pretty sight. As the terrorist screamed for them to deliver Pepper to her, she cried, danced a jig and screamed some more. It was like two or three people were wrapped up into one as she pitched what some recognized as a good, old-fashioned, southern hissy-fit. And it was working! Grown men backed away and gave her room, if not for the threat, then for the entertainment factor.

While the Marines were deciding what defensive action to take against the senior citizen, Jessie Lee stopped her hissy-fit, turned to them, and in her nicest voice, said, "Please give my cat to me, and we'll be on our way."

At that moment Major Shield, the Depot Provost Marshal, arrived and stepped into the center of the action. At the top of his military voice, he shouted, "AT EASE! It sounds like this lady is here asking about her son. Although she hasn't gone through channels, she IS a lady and will be treated as such! Stand down so that no one gets hurt," he ordered. Then he put his arm around Jessie Lee and escorted her into a nearby office.

If the Military Police thought a speeding car was a threat, they were totally undone when the frail woman turned on the tears. Through them she explained that she had just found out where her beloved tomcat was located and was merely trying to rescue him. Just that very morning, she explained, she had received information that Pepper was being held captive here at Fifth Battalion and that today he was going on something called a Crucible! She had to stop it before he was crucified or she'd have no one to blame but herself, she said, with anguish in her voice, to the nice Provost Marshal.

"Ma'am," began Major Shield, "your son has been safe here with us. This is his final week of training before becoming a Marine. Now, you wouldn't want him to miss out on that after all the hard work he's gone through, now would you?" he asked. He smiled nicely, and Jessie Lee's heart thawed a smidgen. Was it possible that her darling cat had actually gone through recruit training? Impossible! How could that have happened? He was a cat, for heavens sake! Regaining some of her feistiness, Jessie Lee demanded to know, "Where is the General? Why isn't he here to help me? I want action and I want it now!" she warned. "I've endured just about all of this I can stand! Give me my tomcat! NOW!"

The Commanding General, Major General James,

was enjoying lunch at his Quarters One home when the Provost Marshal located him. Apologetic about interrupting his lunch, Major Shield quickly briefed the General on the situation concerning the hysterical woman in search of her tomcat, known to them as Recruit Pepper Parker. The General immediately instructed the Provost Marshal to bring her to Quarters One—on the double!

When Jessie Lee arrived, with her Military Police escort, the Commanding General and his wife welcomed her into their home. After settling her into a big comfortable chair and offering her a glass of sweet tea, the General expressed his concern to the distressed woman that she was not aware of her son's presence in recruit training. He assured her that Recruit Parker had called and left a message on her answering machine the morning he arrived and then followed the phone call up with a required letter. The General had also been briefed that Recruit Parker had written to her on a regular basis while he was in training. He and his staff were well aware of the unusual nature of the recruit, but because he seemed to be adapting to the Marine Corps way of life, the General saw no reason to terminate his training.

"But what about the Crucible?" cried the distraught woman. "I've worked on the base myself and never in my life heard of such a thing! When did they start crucifying recruits?"

The General smiled and gently took her hands in his while he explained why they called the exercise the Crucible.

"You see, Ma'am, this exercise is a test given to see if a young recruit is ready to graduate and defend his country. If he can't successfully complete the Crucible, he will be recycled into another platoon to gain more training so that he can succeed.

"Unfortunately," the General continued, "at this very moment Recruit Parker is on his way to Page Field to participate in the Crucible, and I think it best not to bring him back. Also, it would cause the recruit undue stress if we told him, just at this critical point in his training, that his mother was looking for him."

The General again assured Jessie Lee that her son would not be crucified and that he was safe and sound. When Recruit Parker returned from the Crucible on Saturday, he would direct that he be allowed to call her. Until then, she just had to trust him that her boy was safe. He encouraged her to attend Family Day and Graduation with all the other parents the following week.

Through tears and bouts of sobbing and hiccupping, Jessie Lee listened to what the General had to say.

She graciously accepted the two-day pass the Provost Marshal gave to her and then quietly fainted on the General's sofa.

When Jessie Lee finally opened her eyes, she found herself surrounded by two Navy Medics, the General, his wife and a group of anxious Marines.

The smiling General asked how she was feeling. Jessie Lee was still worried but stood as tall as possible when she again stated that she wanted Pepper. Once again the General convinced her that he was safe and sound. She just needed to go home and await his call. General James ordered his staff to extend every courtesy to Recruit Parker's mother and kindly escort the lady home. But before she left, he invited Jessie Lee to join him at the Colors ceremony at Barrow Hall prior to graduation. She was also invited to join him in the VIP stand to observe her son's graduation.

When Bubba Billy arrived home later that day, Jessie Lee, back home from her emotional experiences at Parris Island, swept him up in her arms and hugged him so hard he thought he'd crack wide open. He knew why she was so happy and pretended that he cared. Of course, he'd known exactly where Pepper was and had just been making the best of a bad situation.

Meanwhile, the gang had been following Pepper's progress throughout his training. After he completed the Crucible and graduated, they planned to give him a hero's welcome home.

Under the present circumstances, Bubba figured it was best if he kept his backpack ready with all his essentials in it in case he had to be away from home for an extended period of time. If things went well for him, his brother would be assigned to some faraway place and not be a contender for the rank of alpha cat of the hood. He knew that Pepper had a score to settle with him, and it wasn't going to be pretty. The alpha cat wannabe wondered, with trepidation, if the Marines had taught his brother any karate.

Chapter 39

THE CRUCIBLE

The Company Commander's inspection had gone well, and the next item on Platoon 5001's agenda was considered to be awesome and unforgiving. They had come so far, this little band of brothers. The preceding weeks of boot camp had drained away every shred of their old identity and replaced it with a self-confidence that inspired them to finish what they had started.

Goal oriented, they knew if they relied on teamwork, they would march home in triumph from the Crucible to a Warrior's Breakfast—but that was in the future. The next fifty-four hours would test them physically, mentally and morally and would be the defining moment of their recruit training.

One recruit in particular had surprised and delighted his drill instructors—Recruit Pepper Parker. After giving up on his "accidental recruit" excuse, Recruit Parker had floated to the top like sweet cream. His can-do attitude and team spirit had been noted, and they challenged him in areas where they knew he excelled—like climbing, night vision and intelligence. He was one of a kind—their secret weapon that would be especially effective during the Crucible.

"It's an OOH-RAH day!" screamed Pepper. "Fifty-four hours of the Crucible and it's 'see the emblem, take the emblem!' Swaggering comes natural now, and this recruit is ready to swing into high gear! Got on his Kevlar helmet, boots and utes and packed his 782 gear. His pal RIP the rifle is hugging Mister Velcro. Let's get to it!" he shouted to anyone who would listen.

It was Day One of the Crucible. The drill instructors were feeling good—like they should—as they conducted the night movement march to the Crucible site. A ghostly fog hung low as eighty-eight boots thumped the ground in unison. Anxious creatures of the night scurried into the safety of the brush to watch and wait until the intruders passed them by.

Staff Sergeant Awesome led the forced march, chanting:

EARLY ONE MORNING IN THE MIDDLE OF THE NIGHT,

TWO DEAD MEN GOT UP TO FIGHT.

BACK TO BACK THEY FACED EACH OTHER,

DREW THEIR SWORDS AND SHOT ONE ANOTHER!

HERE WE GO! ALL THE WAY! EVERY DAY!

When the highly charged platoon arrived at the Crucible site, Pepper could hardly contain himself. Overhearing the drill instructors in their house discussing the operation had enabled him to collect stray information about the Crucible. He was as prepared as a recruit could be. In fact, Pepper was so charged up, the Second Hat threatened to quarterdeck him if he didn't pipe down. He did—but not for long.

After the long trek to Page Field, the platoon settled into their base camp and, following a serious discussion, selected Recruit Parker as their Team Leader. He had an exceptionally sharp mind, his hearing was extraordinary and he could actually see in the dark. Although he was the smallest recruit in their platoon, the majority felt his critical abilities would help all of them get through the Crucible. In return, they could help him with his heavy equipment. After the vote, Team Leader Parker and his teammates devised a plan to present to their drill instructors.

"Sir," Pepper called out. "This recruit was selected Team Leader and he requests permission to speak to Senior Drill Instructor Staff Sergeant Awesome, Sir!"

PERMISSION GRANTED, RECRUIT PARKER, responded the Senior Hat. WHAT'S THIS ABOUT?

"Sir, these recruits are good to go when it comes to a party in the woods. We've got our strategy mapped out for the Crucible. This recruit requests permission to brief the Senior Drill Instructor."

GIVE ME A COPY OF YOUR PLAN, said the Senior Hat. I'LL GO OVER IT WITH SERGEANTS SKITTLES AND CLIFTON AND THEN YOU MAY BRIEF US ON HOW YOU PLAN TO PROCEED.

After a short discussion, the Junior Hat called the platoon into a school circle, and Recruit Parker briefed their strategy.

"On Event One," began Pepper, "our team will fly across those two horizontal logs at Private First Class Jenkin's Pinnacle—a piece of cake! We'll climb over the Swinging Beam riki-tik with everyone helping with the equipment. Tonight this recruit has volunteered as the point, reporting back the enemy's location and plan of attack to the drill instructors and S-2. The enemy will be crying for mercy while we're running to the Reaction Course for Event Two!

"At Private First Class Garcia's Engagement we'll start hitting 'em high and low with the pugil sticks. Then, while we're resting, we'll participate in a warrior case study about Private First Class Garcia—a good Marine!

"Following the Crucible's schedule, this recruit and his team will then race to Sergeant Basilone's Challenge where they'll help each other over the eight-foot high log obstacle.

"When these recruits reach Event Two," continued the fired up recruit, "their spirits will still be high, adrenaline racing through their bodies. The next three-hour event will challenge them to use three wooden boards to cross a bunch of stumps without touching the ground. We'll do that riki-tik, and then these recruits will negotiate a water hole using the same wooden boards to get across.

"The next challenge will be to transport a large container over a wall. This obstacle will require a lot of strength, but the bigger recruits will support the smaller ones. We'll all be stretching our new muscles to keep the container from falling.

“The pugil stick battle might take a toll if we suffer any ‘killing’ blows, but if there are any, we’ll take our wounded with us.

“Event Three will test our strength and fortitude when we have to complete Noonan’s Casualty Evacuation by rescuing the downed pilot. But this team is confident we can get the job done. At the Enhanced Obstacle Course this recruit volunteers to be ‘shot’ by the sniper because he’ll be lighter for his teammates to carry on the stretcher.” Pepper stating the obvious made the drill instructors smile. They knew that they would decide who the ‘killed’ recruit would be, and it wouldn’t be the lightweight. But Pepper’s suggestion sure showed the little recruit’s intelligence.

Pepper took a deep breath and continued his brief. “These recruits will then strap on their NBC goggles, and this recruit will lead the team in reconnoitering the area for the Night Observation Course. We’ll be listening to the night sounds, sneaking around like cats on the hunt, and then I’ll report our observations to the S-2!”

WELL DONE, remarked the Senior Hat when Pepper finished briefing the plan. YOU AND YOUR TEAMMATES NEED MORE WORK IN A FEW AREAS, BUT THE PLAN SOUNDS LIKE A GOOD ONE.

"Sir, thank you, Sir," grinned the little recruit.

Before the recruits of Platoon 5001 fell asleep on the first night of the Crucible, their drill instructor held a class on Marine Corps Core Value, HONOR.

As the Series and Company Commanders readied their own sleeping area, a Marine officer stepped out of an official green sedan that had been parked nearby. He approached Captain Boucoup and First Lieutenant Chevron and asked to speak with them.

"Good evening Captain Smith. What brings you out to the boondocks this fine evening?" Captain Boucoup asked, with not a small amount of apprehension.

"Sir," the visitor began, the Commanding General asked me to deliver a message to you."

"And what might that be?" asked Captain Boucoup.

"I'm here on urgent business," the General's Aide responded. "Do you have a recruit here by the name of Pepper Parker?"

Instantly on alert, the Company Commander positioned himself between his men and the General's Aide. "Yes, I do. Is there a problem? Recruit Parker is involved in the Crucible. This is not a good time to deliver news of any kind—good or bad! Can it wait until we return to base on Saturday?" asked Captain Boucoup.

"It's your call," replied the Aide, "but the General wants Recruit Parker to call his mother as soon as possible. There appears to have been a mix-up in the enlistment papers, and she's been on the warpath. It seems that Recruit Parker is a cat—her adopted pet. He shouldn't be training as a Marine."

Captain Boucoup didn't know whether to laugh or cry! The little recruit had been telling them from the beginning that he shouldn't be there, persistently labeling himself an accidental recruit. "Well, doesn't that beat all," he sighed. "I guess it's true that the recruiters need to 'make mission,' but we can't blame this one on them! Somewhere out there is an enlistee by the name of Danny Parker; but that's a problem for another day.

"Please tell the General that Recruit Parker has adapted to the Marine Corps way of life and that I believe he's just too close to the finish line to deny him what he so richly deserves. At the end of the Crucible, for better or worse, I'll personally see to it that he calls his mother. It's only another day and a half. Recruit Parker has earned the chance to graduate, whether he planned to or not."

"Sir, the General thought you might say that, and

he agrees," said the Aide. "Just make sure that the recruit calls his mother as soon as possible. She's one fired up female, and we don't want another episode. The news media have been all over this. We just want to keep everyone happy."

"Enough said, Captain Smith. I'll make the arrangements for a phone call as soon as we return to base," Pepper's Company Commander replied.

Event Four of Day Two held a busy schedule for Platoon 5001's band of brothers. Reveille at 0400 came much too early, but they forced their exhausted bodies towards the challenges of a new day. The accidental recruit was already busy going over strategy with the drill instructors.

"Sir," Recruit Parker began, "these recruits are tired all over. Combat Assault Re-Supply won't be a walk in the park, but we'll git 'er done! We'll pull ourselves up those ropes and, with teamwork, climb that 10-foot wall and slide down the other side. Did this recruit tell the drill instructor that he likes to climb?" asked Pepper.

"With our bayonets fixed, we'll crawl and tunnel under the barbed wire through the mud and the blood. Then we'll take some butt strokes over to Event Five. We'll drag the dummy from the top of that 18-foot tower of the Skyscraper, then move on to the

Stairway to Heaven. Our team will carry the ammo and water cans over the ladder obstacle, then head for the Weaver, where we'll use our collective brains and brawn to get through the Combat Endurance Course.

"Sir, these recruits' butts will be dragging, but Sergeant Gonzales' Crossing will be waiting for us to scale the ropes with our gas masks on, and we wouldn't want to disappoint him.

"At Event Six the platoon will give live fire at Corporal Day's Defense, and then, in honor of Corporal Jason Dunham's Medal of Honor, we'll master our specialty, the Night Infiltration Course.

"Sir, this platoon will be a bunch of tired puppies, but we'll make you proud! We'll finish the Crucible with time to spare," bragged the little recruit on behalf both of himself and his teammates.

At the end of Day Two, the ragged recruits didn't have any time or energy to spare, but that evening they listened attentively to the Senior Hat lecture on Marine Corps Core Value, COURAGE. And then, just for fun, the Hats took them on a five-mile run:

OH YEAH! HERE WE GO!

A LITTLE RUN JUST FOR FUN!

MILE ONE! JUST FOR FUN!

MILE TWO! JUST FOR YOU!

MILE THREE! JUST FOR ME!

MILE FOUR! GIVE ME MORE!

MILE FIVE! I'M ALIVE!

After the motivational run, heaving a collective sigh that could be heard all the way back to main side, the exhausted recruits fell asleep at 2300 and slept well.

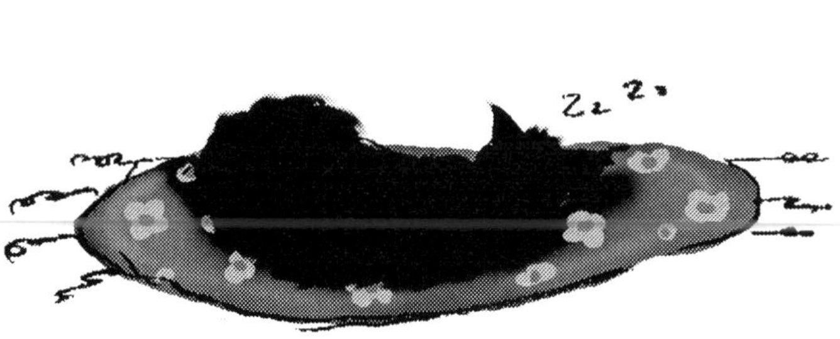

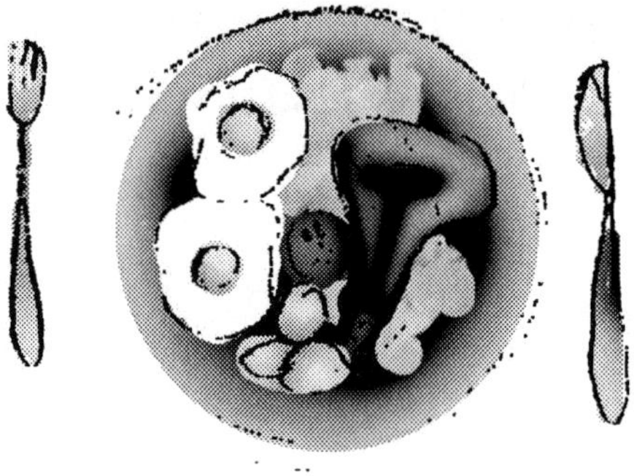

Chapter 40

A JOB WELL DONE

Day Three, 0300 and Platoon 5001's forty-four recruits were running on low-level lights. In spite of their feet having blisters on top of blisters and their bodies scratched, bruised and ready to keel over, they were highly motivated. WARRIOR'S BREAKFAST HERE WE COME! they cried, as they began the long march back to base.

In their midst, Recruit Parker was so fired up he thought he would explode! "Just nine more miles and that steak has this recruit's name on it!" he sang. He joined the rest of the joyful band of brothers proclaiming, WE CAME, WE CONQUERED AND WE FINISHED TOGETHER! OOH-RAH MARINE CORPS! RING THE BELL! MISSION ACCOMPLISHED!

"Does that Marine Corps emblem have this recruit's name on it?" yelled Pepper. "Oh, YES! Life is good! Is that my Warrior's Breakfast calling me? Recruit Par-ker-r-r, come and get it!"

While the Hats led their platoon from the Crucible

site to the Iwo Jima memorial, they all chanted:

FIRST PHASE, IT BROKE ME DOWN.

SECOND PHASE, I STARTED TO COME AROUND.

THIRD PHASE, I WAS LEAN AND MEAN.

GRADUATION, STANDING TALL IN MY GREENS!

TO ANYBODY WHO ASKED ME WHY,

HERE'S THE DEAL, HERE'S MY REPLY:

I'LL BE A MARINE 'TIL THE DAY I DIE.

The Marine Band and Color Guard were waiting at the replica of the Iwo Jima Monument when the weary Crucible survivors arrived. The tired but joyful recruits dropped their gear in neat piles and formed around the monument for the Colors ceremony. They listened attentively while the chaplain thanked God for helping the recruits through the Crucible and spoke about all the difficulties they had overcome. Then he prayed they would be worthy of the honor they were about to receive.

The Company First Sergeant spoke next, telling the recruits they were about to join an elite company. He pointed to the statue depicting real men—four Marines and a Navy Corpsman. The First Sergeant cautioned the recruits never to tarnish the heroes' memory.

After the Color Guard raised the flag and departed, Senior Drill Instructor Staff Sergeant Awesome commanded the platoon to stand at ease. This was the moment they had all been waiting for: THE EMBLEM CEREMONY! Within moments, they would be REAL Marines!

Moving down the line , the Senior Drill Instructor stopped and faced each recruit individually. He pressed the treasured Marine Corps emblem—a small black metal eagle, globe and anchor—into the recruit's left hand, saying, "Well done, Marine." After shaking his right hand, the Hat then moved on to the next recruit. This was the only time a Marine's tears were ignored.

When the Senior Hat came to Recruit Parker, he was almost in tears himself. This particular recruit had presented him and his drill instructors with a truckload of unique challenges, but Parker had finally settled down to the task of becoming a United

States Marine. If the Hat knew that the young Marine standing before him was, indeed, an accidental recruit, he didn't mention it.

The Senior Hat took great satisfaction in telling the recruit, GOOD JOB, MARINE, while he pressed the emblem into the accidental recruit's paw. He also told him that he would be tracking his progress in the Marine Corps and invited Pepper to keep in touch with him. If the new Marine ever needed help, Staff Sergeant Awesome would be only a phone call away. United States Marine Private Pepper Parker thanked the Senior Drill Instructor.

AND BY THE WAY, RECRUIT, said Staff Sergeant Awesome with a smile, YOU'VE EARNED THE RIGHT TO A PHONE CALL TO YOUR MOTHER AFTER THE WARRIOR'S BREAKFAST.

"Sir, thank you, Sir," beamed the little Marine.

After drying their tears, the proud Marines of Juliet Company, marched to the mess hall for their well-earned Warrior's Breakfast. They were sliding and gliding but began a loud rhythmic stomping when they reached the mess hall. A light-hearted Pepper joined the rest of his platoon as they called out "Good morning, ladies!" to the platoon of new recruits who were trying to eat their breakfast in eleven minutes.

With great anticipation, the accidental Marine

heaped his tray with delicious steak, potatoes, grits and biscuits dripping with real butter. He smacked his lips and purred while he attacked the food from heaven. After twelve weeks of people food, Pepper wasn't sure he would ever want to go back to the dried cat food Jessie Lee doled out. He didn't feel like a cat anymore; he felt like a United States Marine! And that Marine would be talking with his mistress in a matter of hours. "Life is good," purred the cat.

RING
RING

Chapter 41

AN ANSWERED PRAYER

Pepper's mistress, Jessie Lee, was waiting by the phone when it rang late Saturday morning. She couldn't believe that she had finally found her adopted tomcat. And he was going to be a real Marine! She knew Pepper was smart, but his drill instructors had to have been supermen to have made a Marine of him. She wasn't sure she could forgive the General or his men for putting her through such a devastating experience, but she would think about it. The most important thing was that Pepper was safe, and she was about to talk with him!

"Hello, Mama Cat," Pepper began. "I'm sorry I haven't been able to get in touch with you, but the most exciting thing has happened! Did my drill instructor call to tell you?" he purred.

Jessie Lee was so choked up she couldn't even talk. She had her boy on the phone, and all she could do was cry like a baby.

"Are you all right?" she asked through her tears. "I've been so worried about you and searched everywhere. I heard some talk about an unusual recruit at Parris Island, but that happens all the time. In fact, there was a famous boxer who tried to go through training, but he didn't make it!

"Pepper, I'm so happy to hear your sweet voice! Did they feed you all the things you like and not disturb you while you were napping? There are so many questions and things I want to say. I can't wait to see you," Jessie Lee sobbed. "If I'd known where you were, I'd have been there in a nanosecond to get you."

"I know," Pepper replied. "But that was then and this is now. You probably won't recognize me anymore, but I'll pick you out of the crowd, so don't worry. I'll be home soon and tell you all about it."

"But the General says I can't see you before Family Day next Thursday," Pepper's mistress complained. By this time she was sobbing and hiccupping so much it was hard for her to talk.

"I know, and I'm just fine, Mama Cat," Pepper continued to purr in his best military voice. "It's a long story. I'll tell you all about it when I see you next Thursday. Until then, just know I love you and can't wait to see you.

"Jessie Lee, my drill instructor just called me to formation, so take good care of yourself, and this recruit will see you soon. I love you with all my heart," Jessie Lee's tomcat declared.

When the phone call ended, Jessie Lee took a deep breath and cried like a baby. "How could this have happened?" she kept asking herself. Herself didn't have an answer.

ROOT BEER

Chapter 42

HAPPY DAYS ARE HERE AGAIN!

By the following Wednesday evening, Jessie Lee was almost finished with preparations for Family Day and Pepper's graduation at Parris Island. She treated the Catmobile to a custom wash job and gassed it up to the brim with High Premium Extra Gold just in case things didn't go as planned, and she needed the extra power. Then she placed the special guest boarding pass in the car's window indicating that she was all legalized to go on the base. All systems were go for the car!

Then it was time for the little old lady to do the impossible—find something decent to wear to the festivities. It wasn't going to be easy, because when she'd retired ten years ago, she had framed and hung her retirement certificate from the Federal Civil Service and gone "casual" in every sense of the word.

In an attempt to divorce herself from the fast lanes of Shirley Highway and the Beltway around D.C., Jessie Lee had packed away all of her career memorabilia and "other life" clothes. She had shoved most of the boxes under the big four-poster bed. What was left over was probably stored somewhere in the attic.

No more business suits, high heel shoes or briefcases for Jessie Lee. Tennis shoes, soft running outfits and hats displaying logos of the Washington Redskins and Carolina Panthers now filled her closets. Jessie Lee knew that recruit graduations always brought in families from all over the world. There was bound to be someone there who would recognize her from her days at Headquarters Marine Corps, and she wanted to look nice.

First, she emptied the nightstand and dresser drawers searching for her Merle Norman make-up. She had all but forgotten how to put on her face, but figured it would be like riding a bicycle—something you didn't forget how to do.

Then, with a grimace, Pepper's mistress prepared to revisit the boxes that held her discarded clothes and memories of a past life. Sipping from a tall glass of sweet tea, she thought about all the places she had worn the clothes as she visited the boxes one by one.

In the first box she found suits and memorabilia worn and collected during her assignment in South Korea. For a year she had worked for Eighth Army

G-2 Intelligence and shivered as she remembered the bitterly cold winter.

Her 1971-1973 Vietnam adventure had proven to be more exciting and a lot more dangerous. Before returning to the Real World, she had witnessed the arrival of helicopters bearing their precious cargos of freed American prisoners of war. She remembered standing outside her quarters at Tan Son Nhut Air Force Base, waving and shouting to them as the helicopters swooped in for a landing. What a glorious sight! Such a long time ago, but it seemed like yesterday.

After drying her eyes, Jessie Lee sorted through the lovely long gowns she'd later worn at various parties and Marine Corps Birthday Balls—all out of date and certainly not appropriate for Family Day.

Although the awakened memories were mostly good, a trip down memory lane, a blast from the past, wasn't on today's agenda.

Jessie Lee was grabbing for the last box under the far side of the bed when her hand came in contact with an unexpected object. It was warm and hairy and, with a loud hiss, it bolted from beneath the bed when she touched it. The surprise discovery caused her, instinctively, to bring her head upward, and she almost knocked herself out when it slammed against the bed slats. Her cheek connected with the edge of a nearby box as she tried to scoot out from under the bed.

"Horse feathers!" she groaned as she ran her hand over her head and face, checking for damage. "All the new clothes in the world won't help me if I'm sporting a black eye or a big lump on my head."

Slowly inching her way from under the bed, Jessie Lee tried not to laugh or cry. The fact that she ended up in such unbelievable and sometimes hard to explain situations was something she seemed to do on a regular basis—without even trying.

With the exception of a large painful lump on the back of her head and a tender spot near her right eye, she had escaped without any major damage. Catching movement out of the corner of her good eye, she had a brief glimpse of Bubba Billy sitting near the bedroom door. Then he was gone without so much as a wave of his tail.

After trying on several old business suits with laughable results, Jessie Lee drove downtown to the Yellow Lily Boutique. After several hours spent coaxing the new clothes to fit her old retired body, she settled on a nice casual outfit of camel colored slacks with a black leather jacket and matching hat. Pepper had offered to show her around the base where the Marines had held him captive, so she added a nice pair of walking shoes to replace the well-worn sneakers.

The next morning she began packing a huge picnic lunch for Pepper and his friends. Bubba Billy and all the Pet Pals would be there. Pepper had also mentioned that Recruit Skippy would be joining them.

Gently layering the dumplings into the huge pot of bubbling chicken broth, Jessie Lee smiled. Grits and chicken n' dumplings were the only human foods Pepper liked, so she had to be sure there was enough to go around. She filled ten gallon-size, zip-lock bags with shrimp and crab meat. Then filled ten more with her boys' favorite crunchy pet food. Pepper, Bubba Billy and the Pet Pals would be in hog heaven diving into all the bags of Science Diet, Iams and a new mystery treat she had found. It was all ready to be loaded into the Catmobile the next day. "Pepper will gain at least ten pounds before seven o'clock comes around tomorrow night," she chirped as she pumped both arms into the air with glee. Anticipating the best, but planning for the worst weather, the excited senior citizen loaded the Catmobile with containers of Skin-So-Soft, umbrellas, blankets and fold-up chairs. To be on the safe side, she took just about everything that wasn't nailed down.

Welcome Home P2!!!
CATMOBL
Welcome Home P2

Chapter 43

FAMILY DAY

The next day, when the big white Eldorado approached the Parris Island main gate, the Marine sentry came to attention and saluted smartly as he motioned the lady to pass through. Jessie Lee gave him a sassy salute right back and smiled as she gunned the Cadillac up to the full forty-five mile per hour speed limit. As soon as she cleared the gate, the sentry called the Officer of the Day to alert him that Ms Parker had arrived. VIP protocol was set in motion

Although Jessie Lee had arrived early, it appeared that at least a thousand other families had the same idea because a parking space was hard to find. Luckily, a young Marine Captain wearing a shoulder rope came out of nowhere and guided her to a reserved parking space right in front of the Liberty Building. The General's Aide-de-Camp helped her out of the car and then, taking her arm, escorted her to a special reserved seat. Jessie Lee didn't know it at the time, but her seat faced dead center of the area where Pepper's platoon would be positioned. A handsome Marine Master Sergeant soon took the seat beside her.

The bleachers behind her and to the sides were filled with other recruits' family members, and the roar of happiness was music to her ears. To Jessie Lee, it was pure joy to see so many happy people under one roof—and she was one of them! Within twenty minutes they would each find their special Marine and hug him or her like they'd never been hugged before. The families were happy, the Marines were in high spirits and the drill instructors were guardedly thrilled. The drill instructors looked forward to meeting the young Marines' families that had supported them throughout their training and driven long distances to be with them in this treasured moment. Life is good but, this was better than good—this was as good as it gets and then some!

Private Parker's mother was being treated so nicely that she had a flicker of remorse about the way she'd crashed the main gate just last week and created a scene. But some days you ate the bear and other days the bear ate you. Today she was having some tasty bear meat and it tasted oh so good!

Unlike many of the other parents, Jessie Lee was sure she'd recognize Pepper, because he would be the only one walking on all fours. It was going to be interesting to see how the drill instructors had managed to keep Pepper in training without laughing themselves silly.

While she was waiting, Jessie Lee mentally reviewed her list of all the reasons her sweet tomcat couldn't possibly be a Marine. First, where had they found a small enough uniform that would also accommodate Pepper's long tail? Second, what about his whiskers? Did they shave them off? Third, the skinhead haircut! If they had put a single nick on Pepper's scalp she would be in front of the Commandant's desk so fast it would make his head spin. Surely he didn't know what was going on at Parris Island or he would have put a stop to the pranks! Still, General James didn't seem too concerned about Pepper's appearance when she'd chatted with him last week. In fact, he and his entire staff had acted as though her cat was just one more recruit. "Are they really that hard up to find recruits," she wondered, "or was there something else they weren't telling her?

"Well, it's all going to be made perfectly clear in just a little while. I'll be able to hold my boy and inspect him myself for any signs of abuse. If there are any, the Marine Corps will find out what a fired up mother can do, and she'll do it long before the sun goes down!"

While waiting for one o'clock to come, Jessie Lee and the other family members watched a video about yellow footprints and the Crucible. Afterward, a lady sang a pretty song about putting a proud Marine Corps sticker on the bumper of her SUV.

Then it was TIME! The three outside doors opened to a burst of cheers from the families. Fifth Battalion's Juliet Company Marines marched smartly through the doors and lined up in front of the rows of bleachers. Next, their drill instructors glided in and stood in front of them. Jessie Lee desperately looked for Pepper but didn't see any recruits on all fours. Where could he be? Did the General lie to her when he assured her that Pepper would be at graduation? Was he going to be led in on a leash of some sort?

Just like they'd rehearsed, the Company First Sergeant took front and center and asked everyone to stand while the Colors were posted. After they were again seated, he introduced the drill instructors of the three platoons. Jessie Lee's heart was beating so fast she thought she was going to pass out again, but she just had to put on her big girl panties and deal with it. It wouldn't be long now, and she didn't want to embarrass Pepper. She just wanted to hug that precious cat and take him home or at least to a picnic.

As soon as the introductions were made, the

First Sergeant gave the long awaited order to the Senior Drill Instructors to dismiss the troops. They each whirled on their heels and called out, TROOPS DISMISSED!

Taking a deep breath, Jessie Lee immediately screamed, “Pepper! Come here and give your Mama some sugar!” She didn’t have to wait, because a little recruit raced towards her as soon as the word “dismissed” was out of the drill instructor’s mouth. At least she hoped it was Pepper. She was hugging and being hugged by a little recruit. Tears of relief and joy streamed down her face, messing up her make-up and leaving black drippy mascara rings around her eyes. Her right eye was already getting black and blue from her escapade under the bed. That shiner was going to be a real beaut.

Jessie Lee finally took a deep breath and inspected the little Marine she was hugging. He didn’t look like Pepper but her motherly instinct told her that it was Pepper all right. The terrible ordeal was finally over.

As she took in his high and tight haircut and camouflage uniform, she was amazed. “Well! Butter my butt and call me a biscuit, look who’s here!” she exclaimed. They had taken her tomcat and made him into a Marine Cat! And that Marine would belong to her from one-thirty to seven o’clock that evening!

Admittedly, the thought had already crossed her mind that she could hide him in the Catmobile and take him straight home. But the General's Aide was still watching and smiling as though he was reading her mind. Also, the nice Marine Master Sergeant seemed to have joined their little group.

Jessie Lee's eyes widened suddenly when she looked at Pepper more closely. It had just dawned on her that he wasn't on all fours! He was standing upright, looking just like the other Marines! "How could this have happened?" she wondered as she fell into another bout of laughing, hiccupping and sobbing.

Pepper took her hand in his paw and whispered in her ear that his Gullah friend, Madam MoJoe, had taught him how to use secret sheaths to hide his whiskers and tail in order to make him look taller. Trying to get her to smile, he popped his whiskers out and back in again several times. Jessie Lee laughed so hard she almost peed her panties, but she didn't care. Pepper was safe, and her prayers had been answered, making her one happy mama.

Looking up, she smiled in recognition as Madam MoJoe appeared beside her and joined in the hugging party. Pepper basked in the warmth of the reunion. Even in his dreams he hadn't expected Jessie Lee to be there all dressed up and acting as though he was the most precious cat on earth. After his unfortunate incarceration and the long painful weeks without hearing from her, he'd resigned himself to the fact that she'd disowned him. That hadn't happened! She still loved him and now his world was absolutely purr-fect!

The little Marine's world became even better when the large group of his Pet Pals, who had been squatting on the highest bleachers joined them. Pepper's animal friends were all sniffing and licking him, insuring that he carried their scent so everyone would know he belonged to them. Pepper shared high-fives with the males and whispered more than a few sweet promises into Fluffy's ear. As soon as Private Skippy joined Pepper and Jessie Lee, the entourage climbed into the Catmobile and headed for the picnic area.

When the picnickers arrived at Horse Island, they found Ricky Raccoon sitting in the middle of a table he'd reserved for them, licking his lips, thinking about the gastronomical orgy to come. There wouldn't be any unauthorized cigarettes or booze, but root beer was always on the Pet Pals' short list of favorite drinks.

Beaufort Gazette
Miracle at
Parris Island!!

Chapter 44

THE GOOD NEWS AND THE BAD NEWS

The whereabouts of Jessie Lee's cat wasn't a secret anymore, because it was the lead news story in the local Beaufort Gazette and Hilton Head Island Packet. Stations WTOC, WCIV and WJWJ were telecasting every detail of the "Miracle at Parris Island." CNN was on its way, giving moment by moment "breaking news updates" to Wolf Blitzer.

The news media described how Ms Parker had found her missing pet at the Parris Island Marine Corps Recruit Depot. Pepper had become an accidental recruit and the drill instructors had accomplished an amazing feat in transforming him into a Marine. Private Parker had just finished the Crucible and would be graduating on Friday.

The newspaper articles and television programs went on to say that because of the unusual nature of the recruit, the base had heightened security. The Recruit Training Regiment Logistics Officer had ordered additional bleachers to accommodate

Private Parker's large contingent of family and friends. In addition to the families of the other graduating Marines, it was expected that the bleachers would be filled to overflowing with the national press and crowds of curious spectators.

The Parris Island Public Affairs Officer neither confirmed nor denied the stories about the special recruit, referring all inquiries to Headquarters Marine Corps. At this point one might say that "the cat was already out of the bag."

After the grand picnic and tour of the base, Jessie Lee reluctantly returned Pepper and Private Skippy to the Marine Corps. It was exactly seven o'clock and not a second sooner.

By the time she arrived home from Family Day, the neighborhood had been decorated from one end to the other with all things Marine Corps. Her entire family, friends from church, neighbors and members of the local AMVETS Post were in a party mood now that Pepper had been found. They had all joined together to prepare the neighborhood for Pepper's grand homecoming the next day, following graduation. Crimson and Gold Marine Corps flags flew from every house, and big yellow ribbons adorned the magnolia and live oak trees.

Big Bill from the AMVETS, a retired Marine,

was the chef in charge of feeding everyone. He'd already called the local shrimpers to provide lots and lots of shrimp for boiling and for the traditional Frogmore Stew. He would fry up a turkey, and there would also be plenty of broiled soft-shelled crabs, steamed oysters, hamburgers and hotdogs with all the trimmings—a banquet befitting a new Marine.

Before setting up his grill and turkey fryer, Big Bill had cut the grass, deadheaded the flowers and pruned all the shrubs around Jessie Lee's little house. Bill knew she would be tickled pink. He loved to see his old friend smile.

Having felt the poor lady's pain when her beloved cat had gone missing, everyone had helped in the search for him. Now that Pepper had been found, it was time to celebrate and let the good times roll!

It appeared that everyone was at Jessie Lee's house helping with the preparations—with the exception of one. Pepper's brother, Bubba Billy, was conspicuous by his absence.

Ricky, Jesse, Fluffy, Francine, Marvin, Wendy, Patrick and Winston joined the other Pet Pals at the festivities. They watched in fascination as Pepper's mistress danced and frolicked with the well-wishers who had come to help prepare for tomorrow's homecoming celebration.

The Pet Pals had known all along where Pepper had gone, but because he didn't appear to be in harm's way, there had been no need for them to interfere or tell on him. If he had been in danger, his buddies would have simply declared all-out war on the Marine Corps and been done with it.

At the moment they were loudly contributing to the festive mood by making whatever their species' happy sounds might be. The dogs danced, joyfully wagged their tails and barked their approval. The cats meowed, purred and trembled, rubbing their tails against the humans as they herded them here and there.

Ricky Raccoon stood on his hind legs and applauded when he wasn't gulping down scraps of food. Jesse, the Border collie, smiled and stayed close to Cousin Danny. Later, the Pet Pals gathered up all the leftover decorations and headed back to the Happy Hideaway to get ready for their own welcome home party. It wasn't every day that their alpha cat came home a national hero.

The Mayor of Beaufort had already called to invite Jessie Lee and Private Parker to join him on his float during Saturday's Christmas Parade. Later that evening they were to be honored guests at A Night on the Town.

The bad news was that Bubba Billy had gone into hiding until everything blew over. Yesterday, after witnessing the fabulous picnic at Horse Island in celebration of Pepper's re-emergence, he knew the jig was up and slunk home, keeping himself hidden.

With a final glance back at the place he'd called home, Pepper's brother strapped on his little backpack and headed across the Woods Bridge toward Hunting Island, a barrier island where a state park was located. Bubba figured it wouldn't be too busy now that the weather was getting cold. The northern snowbirds who were already settled in for the winter months might be good nearby prospects for a handout.

Bubba hiked all the way to the tiny town of Frogmore before he was lucky enough to find a ride. A rusty pickup truck, slowly inching its way onto the road, was headed in the direction of the beach. Bubba leapt into the open bed. When the slow-moving truck neared the entrance to Hunting Island State Park, Bubba jumped off while the old truck continued its lumbering journey toward Fripp Island.

The tired feline had no trouble finding a suitable hiding place under the porch of one of the beach cabins. After stowing his backpack, he set out to explore the possibilities for dinner. The big cat had never had to beg for food before, and he wasn't eager to start now. It was common knowledge that the vacationers who stayed in the beach cabins normally had more food than they needed and would feed any stray animal that happened to be passing by. Sometimes they even took a stray home with them. Bubba wasn't interested in being adopted, but he was hungry. Hard times called for hard choices.

The lonely traveler knew that those humans lucky enough to vacation on the beach would probably be in a party mood, open to the more the merrier. Bubba wasn't in a merry mood, but he pretended to be. After devouring a meatball and a piece of fried flounder and taking a taste of some potent liquid refreshments, he went back to his hiding place under the porch. There he licked himself from tip to toe, curled into a ball and purred himself to sleep. He would worry about the situation with his brother tomorrow or maybe the day after that. For now, life wasn't exactly good, but it was tolerable.

Chapter 45

GRADUATION DAY

For twelve long weeks, the drill instructors had trained the forty-four members of Platoon 5001 in the hope that each would qualify for the title of United States Marine. Some had fallen by the wayside, but the majority of the wannabes had made it through.

Graduation Day was also a special day for Senior Drill Instructor Staff Sergeant Awesome and his assistant Hats, Sergeant Skittles and Sergeant Clifton. Today their chests would swell with pride as their young recruits marched smartly across the parade field to graduate as Marines. Added to the drill instructors' intense pride was the bonus that they would now have more family time. The training schedule was harsh, but the results were gratifying. "That was why God had planted drill instructors on His green Earth!" mused the Senior. Male drill instructors aren't capable of giving birth, but they had birthed Marines out of the babes their mothers had sent to them.

Earlier that morning Jessie Lee had joined the Commanding General at the Colors Ceremony at

Barrow Hall. During the follow-on coffee in his office, the General hinted that Pepper's career as a Marine would not necessarily cease after graduation, but promised that her boy would not be hurt in any way. He had assured her that she would be kept informed about his mission assignments to protect their country.

It wasn't just another Friday morning—it was a GLORIOUS FRIDAY MORNING! IT WAS GRADUATION DAY! The early morning fog lifted as the sun once again laid claim to "PARRIS ISLAND—WHERE THE DIFFERENCE BEGINS!" The large oak trees surrounding Fifth Battalion swayed in the breeze and appeared to bow in salute to the young men who stood ready to march onto the Peatross Parade Field and claim the title, UNITED STATES MARINE.

The Marine Corps Band had begun its musical tribute to the big event. The bleachers were already filled to overflowing with local Marines, the graduates' families and friends. Cousin Danny had arrived from Westfield, Massachusetts, joining Madam MoJoe and an unbelievably large assortment of the Pet Pals who had come to enjoy the show.

The National Press Corps, complete with cameras, microphones and talking heads, worked alongside the local media and the team from Good-To-Go

Video to film and preserve the incredible story about a cat going through training as a U.S. Marine. Everyone there had a story and an opinion about the miraculous feat accomplished by the drill instructors and the cat. It was almost too good to be true. . . but the graduation ceremony was ready to start. . .

Looking very handsome, dressed in his Blue Dress 'A' uniform, Private Pepper Parker's joy was hard to contain. His lips actually moved as he sang along with the band: "Nothing could be finer than to be in Ca-ro-li-na in the mor-or-or-or-ning…."

Private Skippy smiled as he heard his best buddy, Pepper, yowling something that sounded a lot like felines cat'n around in the mourning. "How's it going?" he called to his fellow recruit. "You're sounding a little off-key for such an important day."

"Everything and everyone is just beautiful!" purred the cat. "My mistress and all my Pet Pals will be here to see me graduate, and this cat is going to make them proud! This Blue Dress uniform will make my Fluffy's eyes spin! Oh, by the way, Jessie Lee told me to invite you over to the house after graduation, and she won't take no for an answer.

"Does that Parris Island Marine Band toot sweet or not?" continued Pepper. "Marvin told me the Meowing Sensations and The Detonators' explosive rock n' roll band will be playing at the AMVETS tonight, and this cat is ready to boogie! You'll be going to the party too, so don't forget!" Pepper was entertaining his friend with his low country shag moves when the Senior Hat called the platoon outside to assemble in formation.

"Sir," Pepper called out. "We'll need another set of bleachers to hold all of my family and friends. You see, my father was a traveling man, and he was pro-active in the reproduction scene before his untimely visit to the local neuter/spay clinic."

"Are you saying you signed up for the program, Private?" asked Captain Boucoup, as he joined the formation.

"Sir," replied Pepper. "I support the program! I even have it on my immediate 'To Do' list. Get tutored—not neutered!

"Sir, my mistress, Jessie Lee, Cousin Danny, my brother, Bubba Billy, and the band of Pet Pals are here to witness my graduation! Just check out all the high fives and Cheshire grins in the stands. Poor Jessie Lee is so happy and excited she's boo-hooing all over that Marine Colonel sitting next to her." Then Pepper paused, observing, "He's patting her shoulder, so I guess it's all right. Wait just a minute! Is he holding her hand?

"Naturally, I'll pay for the dry cleaning. It goes with the territory. My motto has always been to 'Mind my manners, play nice and clean up after myself,' right along with treating others with 'Firmness, Fairness, Dignity and Compassion!' HONOR! COURAGE! COMMITMENT! MARINE CORPS!" the young Marine proudly exclaimed.

TIME TO SHOW EVERYONE WHAT YOU'RE MADE OF, MARINES! ARE YOU READY FOR IT? the Company Commander growled.

SIR, YESSIR! yelled the gonna-be Marines.

Lining up adjacent to the Peatross Parade Field, members of Fifth Battalion, Juliet Company, Platoon 5001 inspected each other. Then the three Hats inspected them again and again. The privates noticed there was something different this time. Gone were the Hats' shrill, demanding voices. Instead, the drill instructors politely whispered to the young Marines while pointing out possible uniform misalignments.

Finally, it was Ten-Hundred, the magical hour! Back at the reviewing stand, the Commanding General, his guests and staff joined the family members in rising for the Invocation. Afterward came SOUND ATTENTION and then the ADJUTANT'S CALL.

At the edge of the parade field, Platoon 5001's officers and drill instructors waited to lead their graduates onto the parade field. The Marines would march as one, each taking an exact thirty-inch step and move with a precise swagger. They owned the day!

"There's the Adjutant's Call! Here we go! We're giving it our usual one hundred and ten percent," hissed Pepper. "We're slidin' 'n glidin' across the parade field. The ladies of Lady's Island will be dancing tonight! This recruit will be a UNITED STATES MARINE, and he'll be on the prowl!"

AH LEFT, YOUR LEFT went the familiar cry.

Pepper had seen all the quitters and non-hackers get on a bus for home months ago. At the time he had wanted to go with them. Only a few good men and this cat had made the cut!

The Marine Band led the marching Marines to the front of the reviewing stand. There they halted, executed a right pivot and came to attention. While the Marine Band played the National Anthem, the military saluted as the civilians stood with them, placing their right hands over their hearts, with not a dry eye among them.

The rest of the graduation ceremony became an indelible memory for each of the new Marines, a savored memory that would always bring a smile, even in the worst of times. They listened closely to the orders to SOUND OFF! REPORT—PUBLISH THE ORDER! OFFICERS CENTER!

ALL PRESENT OR ACCOUNTED FOR, SIR! the Juliet Company Commander shouted.

The Regimental Commanding Officer, Colonel Betelnut, wasted no time explaining to the attentive crowd how these Marine graduates would serve and protect their country against all enemies, foreign and domestic. They had been trained, tested and found worthy to wear the uniform of the nation's greatest fighting force—THE UNITED STATES MARINE CORPS!

Just like in their dreams, the new graduates heard the command to PASS IN REVIEW!

Juliet Company Marines executed a perfect left pivot and, with the Marine Band leading them, marched smartly in review. The clapping, whistles and cheers from families, friends, active duty and retired Marines, plus an assortment of press and other Pepper watchers filled the air. The new Marines marched in perfect lockstep. Private Pepper Parker, at the tail end of the formation, blended seamlessly into the marching platoon, purring, "We're marching right behind you, Mr. Drum Major."

LEFT, LEFT, YOUR LEFT, RIGHT, LEFT, YOUR LEFT sounded the familiar words of the drill.

"The National Anthem has never sounded sweeter! I'm ready, willing and able to salute anything that moves! We're graduating, General James, Sir," Pepper, mentally, informed the Commanding General. "Look at these Marines! Have you ever seen such lean, mean fightin' machines? You know your Juliet Company Marines can individually—or collectively—take on any cat or catfight in the universe and still get back in time for chow!

"Our awesome drill instructors have handed out random words of wisdom and guidance we needed to hear, Sir!

"We're looking good, like we should. Watch us do this oblique, General, Sir! We're rockin' and rollin', good to go! Bring it on!"

General James blinked several times, unsure where the voice had come from, but considering the message, it had to have been Private Parker. "Mental telepathy," the General thought to himself. "Just one more quality that will make him an unbelievable asset to the Corps."

Next came the INTRODUCTION OF AWARD RECIPIENTS. Private Pepper Parker joined five other Marines in stepping forward to receive his award from the Commanding General. Unlike the other recipients, Pepper's award was sealed in a small box and wrapped in an equally small Marine Corps flag.

RETIREMENT OF GUIDONS and HONOR GRADUATE PRESENTATIONS followed the presentation of awards.

"Sir," Pepper announced in silence to the General, "the Chaplain has burned the midnight oil praying especially for this Marine. I won't let you, him or the Corps down, Sir! The Regimental Commander made these Marines blush when he told their families and friends how they could run, hide, jump, and leap over tall buildings in a single bound, landing on their feet every time! It's true! All true!"

Private Pepper Parker had puffed himself up to the point that he no longer stood out from the rest of his platoon. He could easily stretch himself up to at least four and a half feet, looking every bit the Marine. His practiced execution of turns and pivots astounded Jessie Lee and the other spectators.

Everyone was requested to rise as the Marine Band played a vibrant rendition of the Marines' Hymn.

Finally, the Commander of Troops delivered to the Marine Corps' newest members of their Band of Brothers, the one command they had waited two months to hear: DISMISSED!

The graduates took one step backward, pivoted and then exploded into the arms of their loved ones.

Private Pepper Parker (now P-3) made a beeline for his mistress and gathered his friends and loved ones close to him.

"What now?" was the first question on everyone's lips. "Can you come home now?" they asked. "Will you have to go to Iraq?" The new Marine didn't know the answers.

Jessie Lee was so puffed up she was about to pass out from pride. Holding onto Pepper, she turned to the Commanding General, gave him a quick hug and told him, "You took my tomcat and gave me back a Marine! Thank you, I think."

The General wasn't accustomed to family members hugging him, but he took it in stride and congratulated Ms Parker on her son's accomplishment. He also assured her that it had been Pepper's hard work that had gotten him through to graduation and reminded her that the Marine Corps had special plans for him. Private Parker would enjoy ten days' leave and then report to Headquarters Marine Corps. Jessie Lee just smiled at General James and thought, "Bless his little heart. Let the games begin!"

The driver opened the door of the green military sedan, and after the Commanding General had taken his place in the right rear seat, they drove off towards Barrow Hall. There was no blue sticker on the vehicle, but the two gold stars on the red flag flying from the front bumper of the sedan left no doubt as to who was inside.

Jessie Lee opened the doors to the Catmobile and made room for everyone. The dogs liked the windows open; and the cats didn't complain. Private Parker took a deep breath and quietly thanked The Big Drill Instructor in the Sky for taking care of him. At this moment in time he couldn't imagine being anything other than a United States Marine.

It was time to go home. . .

EPILOGUE

AT FIRST THEY THOUGHT IT WAS A MISTAKE.

THEN THEY SUGGESTED IT COULDN'T BE DONE.

SOMEONE THOUGHT THE AMERICAN SOCIETY FOR THE PREVENTION OF CRUELTY TO ANIMALS SHOULD BE NOTIFIED.

TWELVE WEEKS LATER, THEY SHOUTED, "IT'S UNBELIEVABLE!"

IN THE END, THEY ALL SMILED AND SAID,

SEMPER FI, MARINE!

THE END of the BEGINNING